ICON IN LOVE

ICON IN LOVE

a novel about Goethe

by Eric Koch

Mosaic Press
Oakville, ON - Buffalo, NY

Canadian Cataloguing in Publication Data

Koch, Eric, 1919 -
    Icon in love : a novel about Goethe

ISBN 0-88962-644-8 HC
ISBN 0-88962-694-4 PB

1. Goethe, Johann Wolfgang von, 1749 - 1832 - Fiction. I. Title.

PS8521.O23I26 1998   C813'.54   C98-932106-1
PR9199.3.K62I26 1998

Published by MOSAIC PRESS, P.O. Box 1032, Oakville, Ontario, L6J 5E9, Canada. Offices and warehouse at 1252 Speers Road, Units #1&2, Oakville, Ontario, L6L 5N9, Canada and Mosaic Press, 85 River Rock Drive, Suite 202, Buffalo, N.Y., 14207, USA.

Mosaic Press acknowledges the assistance of the Canada Council and the Dept. of Canadian Heritage, Government of Canada, for their support of our publishing programme.

THE CANADA COUNCIL | LE CONSEIL DES ARTS
FOR THE ARTS | DU CANADA
SINCE 1957 | DEPUIS 1957

Copyright ©1998 Eric Koch
ISBN 0-88962-644-8 HC
ISBN 0-88962-694-4 PB
Printed and bound in Canada

MOSAIC PRESS, in Canada:
1252 Speers Road, Units #1&2,
Oakville, Ontario, L6L 5N9
Phone / Fax: (905) 825-2130
E-mail: cp507@freenet.toronto.on.ca

MOSAIC PRESS, in the USA:
85 River Rock Drive, Suite 202,
Buffalo, N.Y., 14207
Phone / Fax: 1-800-387-8992
E-mail: cp507@freenet.toronto.on.ca

MOSAIC PRESS
in the UK and Europe:
DRAKE INTERNATIONAL SERVICES
Market House, Market Place,
Deddington, Oxford. OX15 OSF

Table of Contents

Also by Eric Koch...

Fiction

The French Kiss
McClelland and Stewart, Toronto 1969.

The Leisure Riots
Tundra Books, Montreal 1973.
German Paperback Version, *Die Freizeit
Revoluzzer*, Heyne Verlag, Munich. (SF 3522)

The Last Thing You'd Want to Know
Tundra Books, Montreal 1976
German Paperback Version, *Die Spanne Leben*,
Heyne Velag, Munich (SF 3622)

Good Night, Little Spy
Virgo Press, Toronto, and Ram Publishing
Company, London 1979

Kassandrus
Heyne Verlag, Munich 1988 (SF 4542)

Liebe und Mord auf Xananta
Eichborn Verlag, Frankfurt 1992

Icon in Love
Mosaic Press, Oakville, Ontario, 1998

Non-Fiction

Deemed Suspect
Methuen of Canada, Toronto, 1980

Inside Seven Days
Prentice Hall of Canada, Toronto, 1986

Hilmar and Odette
McClelland and Stewart, Toronto, 1995
Jewish Book Award, June 1996
In German: Bleicher Verlag, Gerlingen. February 1998

The Brothers Hambourg
Robin Brass, Toronto, 1997

Preface

On September 3rd, 1985, an advertisement appeared on page 11 of the *Frankfurter Allgemeine Zeitung:*

Beginnings are hard. What is wanted will emerge only slowly.

— Goethe

It was an advertisement for the *New Medical Journal.* The copywriter could easily have used the ancient German saying "All beginnings are hard." But to give it cultural weight he preferred to quote Johann Wolfgang von Goethe (1749–1832), the author of *Faust,* poet, dramatist, scientist, icon.

In the summer of 1821, Goethe found in the Levetzow house in Marienbad a happy family atmosphere and the care and stimulation that he lacked in his house in Weimar.

Ulrike, the eldest daughter, is attractive, slim, with large blue eyes, fair hair and a shapely nose. She has just returned from a finishing school in Strasbourg and loves talking about it. The old Goethe enjoys chatting to this girl of seventeen and learning about the town where he spent his own student days. Ulrike does not know he is a poet and calls him the "great scholar".

Two years later they meet again. At the summer balls, he watches her as she dances past, light in her movements, unaffected, always a little serious; "serene but not gay", as her mother says of her, not without misgivings. Sitting on the terrace, he watches her on the lawn in her becoming tartan dress. The fashion of Walter Scott has spread to the dressmakers as well. To please the "great scholar" she bends down to pick up a few stones to bring to him — "a new addition to the hundred attitudes in which I see her", as he later writes to her mother in all innocence.

Goethe is lured into strange thoughts and still stranger actions. In the words of Thomas Mann it becomes a story of "gruesomely comic and highly embarrassing situations, at which, nevertheless, we laugh with reverence." Mann intended turning this affair into a novel but finally transformed it into his Death in Venice.

Goethe consults a doctor to find out whether at his age, marriage might be detrimental to his health. The doctor puts his mind at rest, probably suppressing a smile with difficulty. Goethe next takes into his confidence his old friend Karl August, who simply laughs at him. "Girls, girls, even at your age!" Goethe assures him he is serious, and the Grand Duke is moved by the sight of this white-haired old man, desperately begging him, like some youth, to act as his intermediary. There is a wild, insane look of hope in his dark brown eyes that normally are so dominating and have often caused him so much trouble. The situation intrigues the Duke and probably appeals to his sense of mischief. If the Olympian wanted to make himself a laughing-stock, why should he try to stop him? On the other hand, the Levetzows might be a welcome addition to Weimar society, and this is certainly more than Goethe's son and his wife have been.

So Karl August pays a formal call on Frau von Levetzow and presents his friend's offer of marriage. At first the lady takes it as a joke. The Duke's sense of humour is known for its lack of subtlety. Karl August, however, promises Ulrike a large pension in the not too improbable event of Goethe dying before her. The mother expresses her anxiety at the almost certain opposition of Goethe's son and his wife and the consequent bad atmosphere in the house. This, too, can be arranged, Karl August assures her, as he will place a house opposite the castle at the disposal of the "young couple".

The mother stresses the age of her "child". Ulrike is nineteen, but the mother at that age was already on the point of divorce. However, Ulrike has never shown the slightest interest either in marriage or in men in general. At least she must be consulted. The offer is certainly an exceptionally honourable one.

(Richard Friedenthal, *Goethe: His Life and Times,* Weidenfeld and Nicolson, London, pp. 464–465.)

Part One

Goethe in His Time

Goethe was born in Frankfurt am Main, but he spent most of his life, from 1775, when he was twenty-six, until he died at the age of eighty-two, in the small town of Weimar in central Germany. Goethe's patron was Duke Karl August of Saxe-Weimar who was eight years younger and, thanks to Goethe's friendship and guidance, became one of the most enlightened rulers in Germany and a model for his relative, Queen Victoria's Prince Consort.

Weimar had six or seven hundred houses, with thatched roofs or wooden shingles, and one imposing building, the ducal residence. This microscopic company town was Goethe's home base.

Goethe was unorthodox. As a boy of seven he had rebelled against organized Christianity. He sometimes said that as a natural scientist he was a pantheist; as a poet, a polytheist; and in his ethical life, a monotheist. His cast of his mind was metaphysical. He thought of the spiritual world as real and there was a great deal of the esoteric in his thinking.

Goethe was also unorthodox in his personal life. To the consternation of the Duke and the Weimar court, he married the working-class mother of their son only when the boy was seventeen. She died in 1816, leaving Goethe a widower for the rest of his life.

Much remains unknown about Goethe's many love

affairs. His passionate ten-year affair with Charlotte von Stein, a married woman, was probably platonic. The former director of the Sigmund Freud Archives in New York, Kurt Eissler, wrote a two-volume psychoanalytic study of Goethe and took the view that Charlotte von Stein's function in his life was primarily that of a psychotherapist, and she helped him make the transition from his *Sturm und Drang* youth to the calm, settled life of a mature poet, scientist and public servant. In Eissler's opinion Goethe had no sex until he met the waitress Faustina in Rome, one of the inspirations of his *Roman Elegies*. By then he was thirty-nine.

Life, Goethe thought, was difficult and painful. It was his duty, therefore, as it was the duty of every artist, to provide beauty and comfort as a counterweight to existential anguish. The artist's job was to uplift and to ease pain. After Goethe had published the tragic *The Sorrows of Young Werther,* one of the most formidable bestsellers in history, he avoided plots for which he could not provide a happy ending. He was a great believer in practical and intellectual self-help. As the author of *Wilhelm Meister,* he invented the *Bildungsroman,* the novel of education and character formation. The greatest character he formed was his own.

Goethe's productivity was spectacular. The complete works, the *Sophien-Ausgabe,* published in Weimar between 1887 and 1919, contained one hundred and forty-five volumes. Twelve thousand letters have survived. There are thirty-seven volumes of diaries. His scientific writings fill fourteen volumes. Many of the people who visited him published their conversations with him. Goethe was also a good draughtsman and had a well-schooled eye for the visual arts generally. He was a systematic collector, especially of rocks and minerals.

Goethe had a close relationship to music, but words came first, music second. He did not respond to Schubert's powerful settings of his poems, and made a largely unsuccessful effort to understand Beethoven's music, while finding his personality too "untamed". Both Schubert and Beethoven revered him.

Shakespeare is box office all over the world, but Goethe is not. His plays do not travel well, especially to English-speaking countries. Even his most famous play *Faust* is rarely produced outside Germany. The French have less trouble with him. The romantic poet Gérard de Nerval, at the age of nineteen, made his reputation as the translator of *Faust* while Goethe was still alive. But the beauty and music of his verse remains difficult to convey, even in French.

The Setting

In the spirit of a serious jest – his own description of *Faust* – and in order, once and for all, to close the Goethe Gap, let us now suspend disbelief and pretend that in 1992, at the age of seventy-three, Goethe received the Nobel Prize for Literature, "in recognition of his many-sided, profound and fruitful activities in poetry, drama, film, radio and television, his mastery of symbolic language and images, for his sense of harmony and unity between all living things and for his tireless efforts to maintain and strengthen positive values".

Let us imagine that on the day the Prize was announced, Knut Johannson, Permanent Secretary of the Swedish Academy, issued this press release:

Near the end of a century which has experienced two world wars and mass murders on an unprecedented scale, it is fitting that the Nobel Prize for Literature should go to Johann Wolfgang von Goethe. We have decided to award the Prize to him because of our hope that his spirit, a positive, hopeful, harmonious and conciliatory spirit, will give the twenty-first century its name – the Goethean age.

Part Two

THE NOVEL

On August 28th, 1749, at mid-day, as the clock struck twelve, I came into the world. The constellation of the stars was propitious. The sun stood in the sign of Virgo and had culminated for the day, Jupiter and Venus looked on it with a friendly eye, and Mercury was well disposed.

(Goethe, *Fiction and Truth*, page 1.)

Diary Entry for July 23, 1823

Whay a day! o dio! I should really cut short these exclamations, but I have never been happier and now the peak of my existence is over. I saw him! No, what am I saying? I saw him three times. I held his hand, I kissed him, and he said beautiful things to me. I have never before been in a state of ecstasy like this! Now I read his works in a completely different spirit and understand them as never before. Now I can see him in my mind's eye and hear his voice. He speaks exactly as he writes. And how beautiful he is, even today. I can't help it – I know it sounds ridiculous – but I have never seen a more beautiful man...There is mildness in his eyes, and fire at the same time. I have never seen anything like it...He looks like the Apollo of Belvedere.

(Lili Parthey, student of the composer Karl Friedrich Zelter. *Goethe in vertraulichen Briefen seiner Zeitgenossen,* Aufbau-Verlag Berlin Weimar 1979, page 149.)

chapter one

The Goethe family had been spared the suffering of many other anti-Nazi families of his generation. His father, Dr. Johann Caspar Goethe, was a wealthy liberal lawyer in Frankfurt, and his mother, who was eighteen when Goethe was born, a member of an old family. In 1932, when Goethe was thirteen, Dr. Goethe thought the Depression would lead either to a left-wing or a right-wing dictatorship. He therefore opened a bank account in Zürich and in 1935 sent his handsome, extraordinarily gifted boy to a boarding school near Basel. He thought that, if necessary, he and his wife, and the younger daughter Cornelia, would follow. In 1938, it was necessary. They rented a small villa in Ascona, near Locarno, on the shores of Lago Maggiore, where a few other comfortable intellectual German émigrés were awaiting the end of the Nazi terror.

In the same year young Goethe went to the University of Zürich to study law, not because he wanted to but rather to please his father. But he was more interested in writing poetry, in reading Shakespeare, in studying biology, chemistry and physics, and, when at home in Ascona, in having long conversations, till late in the night, with the writers and scholars living nearby

In 1942 he wrote his first play, *Götz von Berlichingen* or *The Knight with the Iron Fist*. It was modeled after Shakespeare's historical plays, with the important difference that Goethe dealt with the future, not the past. He wrote it in six weeks, in Ascona.

The play was amazing. In his Swiss exile, the young man foresaw with crystal-clear clarity, two years before it happened, the generals' plot against Hitler which culminated in the abortive attempt on Hitler's life on July 20, 1944. The decent, tough, honest, defiant, rough-and-ready, coarse but incorruptible Götz, a member of the minor aristocracy, was the centre of a web of conspirators against Evil, men from the left side of the political spectrum and the right, from the north of Germany and the south, from the churches and the unions, the educated and the uneducated. Götz had lost his right hand in the First World War and wore a steel prosthesis covered with a leather glove. After the failure of the *coup,* the missing hand became the symbol of the fatal weakness of the good cause.

The play could not be performed until 1946, in Frankfurt. It anticipated Carl Zuckmayer's *The Devil's General,* which dealt with the Faustian bargain (à la Goethe, later) between the ace-flyer Ernst Udet and Göring. When Zuckmayer wrote it he, too, was far removed from the scene, in exile in Vermont.

After completing *Götz,* Goethe wrote his first novel, *The Sorrows of Young Werther.* He later recalled that "it had the effect of a rocket". The book came out in the fall of 1945. This was but a few weeks after Goethe, who had been close to despair throughout the war, was at last able to return to Frankfurt. It made him a world celebrity, at the age of twenty-six. It seemed that everyone shared Werther's sorrows. No other writer, on the German or the Allied side, had succeeded as he had in describing the combination of cynicism and hope, despair and idealism of young survivors who were living, and often starving, in ruined cities. Goethe's Swiss exile had given him the psychological distance necessary, as the critics said, "to get it right". It was the story of a love triangle which ended in the hero's suicide. Goethe later said that he himself was in a state of such acute depression when he wrote it that he made his hero commit suicide to save his own life.

The success of Werther caught the attention of the rising young media magnate Karl Saxe-Weimar, universally known as Karl. He discouraged the use of his surname because he did not wish to create the impression that he wanted to capitalize on his royal connections. While other thrones had toppled, his relatives, descendants of the Saxe-Coburg-Gotha branch in London and Brussels, had retained theirs. Moreover, he did not wish to be reminded, or remind anybody else, of Kaiser Wilhelm II, whose mother Victoria was the daughter of Queen Victoria and her Consort, Prince Albert Saxe Coburg Gotha, and whose father's mother Augusta was *née* Saxe-Weimar.

Karl was deeply affected by Goethe's good looks and radiant

charm, and by his extraordinary gifts as a versifier, and dazzled by his
erudition generally. Always a shrewd businessman, he decided to cash
in on Goethe's fame. Karl offered him an undefined, highly
remunerated position in the upper echelons of his growing Saxco
empire, on the understanding that Goethe would be available to him
personally as a consultant in matters of policy and strategy, and,
occasionally, as a manager of special projects. Saxco would also have
first refusal on all his future publications, both literary and scientific.

Goethe was far from certain that such an arrangement, however
profitable, would be worth the curtailment of his personal freedom.
However, eventually, he accepted because he liked and trusted Karl
and because he thought that experience in business, especially in the
media business, would be beneficial for his development as a person.
The two men formed a close friendship which lasted for almost fifty
years. After the U.N.'s Goethe Commission on the environmental
crisis in the Sub-Sahara had completed its report in 1963, Karl bought
for him a large house and garden in Oberreifenberg in the Taunus
Mountains north of Frankfurt.

It was to be expected that Goethe's relationship with Karl would be
strained at times. Goethe frowned on his friend's occasional
championing of causes, not because he disapproved of them *per se* but
because he thought that Karl was often guided by their popularity
rather than by their inherent merits. To avoid quarreling with his
friend, Goethe occasionally left Germany for a change of scene. In the
early 'fifties, in his existentialist period, which was intense but did not
last long, he spent some time with his friend Jean-Paul Sartre in Paris
and from 1956 to 1958 he took a film crew to Burma and produced a
popular series of television programs, subsequently distributed by
Saxco. After completing the production, he stayed on in Burma for a
few months, writing plays and poetry, studying Buddhist antiquities,
and conducting scientific experiments. He even made one discovery,
in the area of botany, which received considerable attention in the
learned journals. The long visit to Asia had a profound and lasting
effect on his life, adding an Eastern dimension to his thinking and
feeling, and to his art.

Before going to Asia he had completed *Egmont*. In Burma he
finished two other plays, *Iphigenia* and *Torquato Tasso*. *Egmont* came out
of the Resistance, like *Götz*. But he chose a different format. This time
he wanted an operatic dream-play of the kind Strindberg had written.
This is how he described it:

"There was Egmont, a pleasure-loving charmer in occupied Belgium, not a bit interested in political causes. He suddenly found himself in a situation where, to his immense surprise, he was involved in a life-and-death confrontation with the ice-cold Nazi commandant Alba. By the time they met, Alba had already taken steps to have Egmont shot early the next morning, after a *pro forma* trial in the evening. I took great pains not to make Alba a stereotyped Hollywood Nazi, but an interesting, educated upholder of the Nazi system. To conceal his routine brutalities he often uttered platitudes about the way an orderly society should be run, to which no reasonable person could take exception. Egmont's friends warned him against confronting Alba but because of the young man's naive self-confidence he persisted. The whole of the fourth act is devoted to the argument between the two.

"Alba's tone was scathing.

"'You want freedom?' he asks Egmont with biting sarcasm at the beginning of the big scene. 'A beautiful word. And suppose you had it – what would you do with it?' And Egmont cries: 'But *Herr Kommandant,* we have it now! Never has a people been as free as we are now, under your deadly heel. Your tyranny has liberated us. If we depart by a mere fraction of an inch from the way you want us to live, we're arrested and tortured, and, if it suits you, shot at dawn. So we have created our own freedom. We are what we want to be, every one of us. Any time we have a thought which contradicts your picture of us as subhuman vermin – and we have hundreds of such thoughts every day – we proclaim our freedom. The fear for our lives which you instil in us, the fear we carry in our bones, makes us free. You didn't know that, *Herr Kommandant?* Well, now you know it. You have condemned us to freedom.'"

Quite rightly, the audience recognized in these ideas the influence of Sartre, but the ending was pure Goethe. He was not the kind of author who would write a traditional execution scene. Besides, being Goethe, he had to concoct a happy ending. The fifth act was an extension of Strindberg's style, an experimental technique much imitated later. It as a magnificently imagined dream scene, during Egmont's last night, with voices, chorus, music, dance, a multimedia apotheosis.

Goethe was often compelled to impose a happy ending on a story which other writers would have ended differently. There was, for example, the long erotic poem *Diary,* written long after *Egmont* and following a tradition established by Tibullus, from whom Goethe took a Latin epigraph. It is a story about a commercial traveler to whom a young waitress in a country inn is attracted. He is married and had to leave his wife behind. The waitress has never experienced physical love and thinks the time has come to lose her virginity. She promises to go to his room at midnight. To his great delight, she does. He takes her in his arms. They begin to make love. But he is unable to complete the act because he cannot be unfaithful to his wife. The waitress is not unhappy because she does not know what she has missed.

This is Goethe's conclusion:

And since, after all, every type of poetry
Is supposed to provide a moral lesson,
I would like to follow this popular tradition
And confess the meaning of these verses.
We may stumble often throughout the journey of our lives,
And yet, in this crazy world,
Two things can help us cope with our daily problems –
Duty, a great deal, but infinitely more powerful is Love.

In December 1968, *Playboy* published its own version of the poem. The moral uplift of Goethe's happy ending did not suit the *Playboy* ideology. This is *Playboy's* happy ending:

Look, it's a crazy world. We slip and tumble.
But two things, Love and Duty, keep us going.
I couldn't rightly call them hand in glove.
Duty? – who needs it? Trust your Love.

The second of the three plays Goethe wrote in the 'fifties – *Iphigenia* – also had its origin in the Nazi period. It was the first major play since Ibsen's *The Doll's House* in which a courageous woman asserted her independence from men in a manner which made even men admire her. This play established Goethe as a feminist writer long before feminism entered the mainstream. But that was not the reason why it became significant. The reason was its uncompromising moral purity.

Many years before his friend Peter Weiss wrote *Marat-Sade,* Goethe heard that the inmates of the so-called "model" concentration camp Terezin – Theresienstadt – performed plays and the children's opera *Brundibar* and even had an orchestra. These were permitted solely for the purpose of misleading visitors from the Swiss Red Cross. All the performers were later sent to Auschwitz. This gave Goethe the idea of writing a play within a play, set in a concentration camp. Camp inmates waiting for their own death were choosing a play to perform. What kind of play, Goethe wondered, would they pick? The answer – Euripides' *Iphigenia in Tauris*. The subject was a woman, quintessentially pure, who succeeded, without any help from outside, in resisting and defeating Evil. But first they had to adapt it to meet their situation.

The third of the three plays of the 'fifties – *Torquato Tasso* – was untypical because it ended unhappily, with the hero's insanity. The subject was "the artist in society". Tasso, an Italian poet of the sixteenth century, was the nickname of the melancholy, super-sensitive art director in a large advertising agency on Madison Avenue in New York. (A good subtitle of the play might have been *The Outsider Inside*.) He and the CEO had been friends since their days together at Princeton. The work's autobiographical content was self-evident, though Goethe took particular care not to offend Karl when constructing his plot.

Goethe's novel about marriage and adultery, *Elective Affinities,* published in 1979 when he was sixty, was most definitely more to Karl's taste. The concept was highly original, and shocking. The action revolved around a routine sexual consummation – the partners had been married for many years – while each imagined having sex with someone else. The child born of this physical union but emotional adultery resembles not them but the objects of their fantasies. It was a novel about mind–body relationships and the nature of sexual magnetism. Goethe could easily have turned it into as great a bestseller as *Werther,* but he deliberately chose a different tone and format designed primarily for readers who enjoy novels about ideas.

As to his scientific writings, Goethe caused a worldwide debate with a series of books on environmental geochemistry. They demonstrated that microbes dwelling deep in the planetary crust were responsible for creating and arranging rocks, oils, gases, metals and minerals that composed the earth's surface. This basic and original work of Goethe was supported by proof in the early 'eighties that the rich lode of gold in Brazil – in the *Serra Pelada* – was produced by swarms of microbes which, over millions of years, concentrated the gold from jungle soils, rivers and rocks. Most of Goethe's findings were bitterly attacked at first by the older generation of academic geologists, biologists, chemists, physicists and paleontologists. But many of them soon relented and began to treat him with something approaching respect.

In conjunction with his scientific work, Goethe published a volume of *Microbe Sonnets,* of which the famous was *Prometheus.* It also evolved into a play. It was written as a Greek equivalent of *Genesis.* Zeus punished Prometheus for stealing fire from Olympus which he then gave to mankind. For this he was chained to the rocky crests of Mount Caucasus. There, an eagle, sent by Zeus, fed upon his liver. But not for long. Trillions of microbes combined to push the rock into the valley, making it possible for Prometheus to elude Zeus and his eagles and create Man and Woman.

———————

Goethe was unique as a performer on television.

With his silken white hair, his lofty forehead, his prominent cheekbones, his dark-brown, lustrous, luminous, translucent brown eyes, with his heart-warming smile, Goethe's face, the most famous since Einstein's, seemed to have been created for this medium. Indeed, it was through his television programs that he was known all over the world as the Universal Sage. He delivered his masterful commentaries in four languages – German, French, English and Italian – but always with the agreeably homely inflections of his native city Frankfurt. The programs were dubbed into twenty-two languages. Their subjects ranged from Buddha via Galileo to Madonna, from Ramses the Second via Mahatma Gandhi to John Maynard Keynes, from Homer via Descartes to country and western music. The success of his programs was due to the Goethe-touch, the Goethe-tone, to his vitality and originality, to his admirable tolerance of people, ideas, places, languages, and to his capacity to discover surprising connections between seemingly unrelated things.

———————

In 1989, Goethe's lawyers took out an injunction against a Indonesian airline which, without permission, had set his celebrated poem *Über allen Gipfeln* (Above the mountain tops) to rock music and used it in its publicity. Last year they took an action against a Mexican travel agency that did the same thing with *Kennst Du das Land wo die Zitronen blühn?* (Do you know the land where the lemons grow?) and against a chain of Iranian florists who unlawfully appropriated *Sah ein*

Knab ein Röslein stehn (The Boy and the Rosebud).

––––––––

Overshadowing all Goethe's other achievements was *Faust,* or rather *Faust Part One,* which was published a year before *Elective Affinities,* although he had been working on it since he was a boy. By 1992, the year of his Nobel Prize, Goethe had drafted a few scenes for *Part Two,* but, for a number of complicated reasons which he himself did not quite understand, he was blocked. *Part One* was recognized as the contemporary equivalent of Dante's *Divina Commedia,* Cervantez's *Don Quixote,* Shakespeare's *Hamlet,* Proust's *Recherche du Temps Perdu,* and Joyce's *Ulysses.* It was a dramatic poem about a man seeking to experience all the possibilities life had to offer. In *Part Two* Goethe had intended to extend these possibilities from the individual to the entire human race. He was to engage in what one critic was to call a "cosmic game".

The core of *Faust Part One* was the old folk-tale of the tired old scientist who, in order to take a short cut to satisfy his thirst for knowledge, resorts to magic and makes a pact with Mephisto who duly promises to deliver, not only abstract knowledge, but, far more important, concrete experiences. All this in return for his soul. One of these concrete experiences, masterminded by Mephisto, led to the ruin of a young woman named Gretchen. This ancient morality tale, first made famous at the time of Martin Luther, had already inspired Christopher Marlowe and others to deal with a number of fundamental questions. What is really important in life? How do we obtain knowledge, by the scientific method or by intuition, the modern equivalent of magic? Where does Evil come from?

By the time Goethe had begun the first draft of the full-length version, Thomas Mann had already published his enormous, multi-leveled novel *Doktor Faustus.* The time was 1947. Goethe was then nearly twenty-eight, and already with Saxco. Thomas Mann's Faust-figure was Adrian Leverkühn, the mad composer of chaotic music in a chaotic world of which the devil had taken hold – Hitler's Germany. Thomas Mann's son Klaus also wrote a *Faust* -novel in the 'forties, *Mephisto,* a story about a great actor selling out to Göring. It was conceived on a smaller scale than his father's, but it was distinctly more accessible.

One of the important features of the *Faust* legend was that it also raised a mundane, very personal question. Every human being, at one stage or another, has entered into a Faustian bargain, a bargain involving the sacrifice of principle, in order to obtain worldly advantage. Goethe had first witnessed such a bargain in the mid-'thirties when he was fifteen and when most of the boys in his class were in the Hitler Youth. Membership was not obligatory and he himself had managed to keep out. Two of his friends who were in the Hitler Youth agreed with him that the official line about the *Aryan* master race was absurd and that this and other Nazi nonsense was bound to lead to catastrophe. Still, they remained silent, raised their arms in the Hitler salute, went camping in the woods with the others, sang songs around the bonfires, in exchange for good marks at the end of the year from their Nazi teachers. One later joined the resistance against Hitler and was caught and shot. The other worked for the Red Cross and fell on the Russian front.

Goethe decided that he would outdo both Thomas and Klaus Mann. He would write a play, not a novel. He would be shameless and use every theatrical trick at his disposal. He would employ his usual Nabokovian fireworks. The words would be heightened by music, dance, film, and every special effect in the business. Karl and his global Saxco empire would look after marketing, promotion and publicity. The story line would consist of high points in a journey through life, part medieval legend, part popular philosophy, part contemporary satire.

This was the bare plot:

Professor Johannes Faust teaches genetics. He has a number of master's degrees in geophysics, space sciences, mathematical economics and theoretical physics, and a background in Byzantine art. He has read widely in pre-Socratic Greek philosophy.

The date is some time in the 'fifties. The professor, sixty-four and close to retirement, has single-handedly discovered the Double Helix – DNA – the basic building block of all living things. He has, indeed, found the secret of life. But he is too careful, too scrupulous, to publish his discovery before the results of one final experiment are in. Therefore, he leaves the path open to James Watson and Francis Crick, who would receive the Nobel Prize for the same discovery in 1962. It may well be that the real reason why Faust delays publication was that he does not know what to do with his life once he goes public since, inevitably, he would receive the Nobel Prize. It is common knowledge that many scientists never achieve anything after they become, as it were, movie stars. Johannes Faust is afraid that would happen to him.

(Goethe was amused when he read that Francis Crick, after receiving the Prize, prepared the following standardized checklist:

Dr. Crick thanks you for your letter but regrets that he is unable to accept your kind invitation to: send an autograph; provide a photograph; cure your disease; be interviewed; talk on the radio; appear on TV; speak after dinner; give a testimonial; help you in your project; read your manuscript; deliver a lecture; attend a conference; act as chairman; become an editor; write a book; accept an honorary degree.)

While waiting for the results of his final experiment, Mephisto, in full uniform, appears to Faust in a dream. The devil wears a feathered hat. He has a limp. He is worldly, charming, sophisticated, intelligent, amusing. He gives Faust another reason for postponing publication.

"Do nothing with your discovery," he says. "It's not safe in human hands. You know very well what man is capable of. Give it to me and I will show you what life is really about. Come with me – I will give you everything you want. But you have to keep going. If you stop for one single minute and say *Hold it! This is the perfect moment!* The game's up."

The word "soul" is never mentioned. Faust quickly signs. He has to use a drop of blood.

When the old professor wakes up he is, miraculously, rejuvenated, ready to savour life to the fullest. The dream becomes reality. After all, this is theatre, make-believe, naturalism would spoil it. Mephisto is not a crude devil, but Faust's alter ego, the side of him which reasons, doubts, tempts and eggs him on for ever greater efforts, for understanding and experience. Not for a moment does Faust lose his head, stand still and exclaim, "This is the perfect moment!"

(This matter of going on – ever striving, ever working – touched the essence of *Faust Part One*. Although Goethe became the idol of Green Parties and of the environmental movement in Europe and North America, he seemed strangely old-fashioned and conservative in his firm support of the Protestant work ethic.)

Mephisto introduces Faust to Gretchen, with whom he falls in love. It was, more than anything else, the portrait of Gretchen's naive and trusting innocence which made the play so popular all over the world, an innocence strangely out of keeping in the blasé world of the late twentieth century. The purity of Gretchen's love for Faust, just like Marguerite's in Gounod's opera a hundred years earlier, struck a universal chord, and when the devil makes Faust abandon her, and when he makes her kill their child, even the most cynical, worldly-wise theatre-goer choked with emotion. Goethe had written the Gretchen tragedy long before he ever started work on *Faust*. It came out Werther's world after the war, when so many similar tragedies occurred. It was not easy to fit it into the dramatic framework of the whole.

After completing the heart-breaking Gretchen tragedy, how could Goethe launch Faust on the second part of his journey, to play a "cosmic game"?

No wonder he was blocked.

Ulrike remembers:

I met Goethe in 1821 in Marienbad; Mother had taken me from my pension in Strasbourg to spend a few months with her there. At that time Marienbad was still a tiny place, indeed scarcely existed yet, and the house we had taken was nearly the largest and finest. Goethe was also living there, and I can still remember the first meeting very clearly. Grandmother sent for me; the maid said she had an old gentleman with her who wished to see me, and I was not at all pleased with this, for it interrupted me in a piece of needlework I had just begun. When I entered the room my mother was there, too, and she said: "This is my eldest daughter, Ulrike". Goethe took me by the hand and looked at me kindly and asked me how I liked Marienbad. Having spent the last few years in Strasbourg at a French boarding school, and being only seventeen, I knew nothing about Goethe, and what a famous man and great poet he was, so I was quite unembarrassed before this kindly old gentleman, and without any of the shyness which usually overcame me when I made new acquaintances. Goethe invited me the very next morning to come for a walk with him, in the course of which I had to tell him all about Strasbourg and my school. I complained in particular that I felt lonely without my sisters, from whom I had been separated for the first time, and I am convinced that it was this childlike frankness of mine that interested him. For from then on he spent a great deal of time with me. Nearly every evening he took me with him when he went out walking, and if I did not come he brought back flowers for me, and I suppose he very soon noticed that I took no interest in the stones he was often looking at, but apart from this I was willing to learn; towards evening, too, he would

29

often sit by the hour on a bench outside the door, telling me about all sorts of things. When I realised what a great scholar he was, he was already so well known and familiar to me that this could not possibly make me feel shy or embarrassed; and later, too, it occurred to no one, not even my mother, to see in our frequent association anything more than the pleasure taken by an old man who, by his years, could have been my grandfather, in the company of a child, which was after all what I still was. Goethe was such a kind, charming old gentleman, whose friendship a young person could well enjoy, especially when she took so lively an interest in all the things which he described to her in so agreeable a manner: flowers, stones, stars and literature.

(Goethe: Conversations and Encounters, edited by David Luke and Robert Pick, Henry Regnery Company, Chicago 1966, page 111.)

chapter two

onday, October 12, 1992, was a crisp fall day. In the afternoon Goethe went for a little walk along his favourite path. On the northern slopes of the Feldberg, opposite the mountain topped by the ruin of the medieval fortress of Oberreifenberg. He took his time because he had not yet fully recovered from his nearly fatal heart attack in March. No doubt his narrow escape from death explained the manic intensity of his passion for the nineteen-year-old Ulrike von Levetzow, now in her second year at the University of Stockholm, a girl whose idealism and ambition entranced him. Tears came to his eyes as he thought of her uncombed hair and her slightly protruding upper lip which he so desperately wanted to kiss. So far he had only given her avuncular kisses on the forehead and she had usually given him only a respectful peck on the cheek. She called herself his "disciple". Valuable time was passing. Did patience have no limits?

The previous fall he had walked with Ulrike along the same path, They had breathed in the same autumnal smell of burning compost which once again the wind blew over from the nearby fields, that agreeable, highly evocative smell he remembered nostalgically from his own childhood, when, on Sundays in the fall, his mother took him and Cornelia to the Taunus, a Sunday occupation for so many Frankfurters. He had told Ulrike the roots of the word "compost", making a silly joke – "it's named after a great composer who composed melodious compost" – to convey to her that even icons could be silly.

It was already two long years since the summer of 1990 when the symptoms of his passion for her first appeared. It was in Baden-Baden, in the dining room of the small, quiet Hotel Süss, just off the Lichtenthaler Allee, when he was surprised to discover that he could not take his eyes off her and that his heartbeat accelerated dangerously whenever they met in the lobby. Then Ulrike was only seventeen. She was with her attractive mother Amalie von Levetzow and two younger sisters. They were a German family living in Sweden.

Amalie was the socially ambitious daughter of a department store owner in Hanover, a voluptuous, elegant beauty. Ulrike's father was a steel industrialist in Düsseldorf who had divorced Amalie in 1988, giving her a generous settlement. By now Amalie and her three daughters had been living in Sweden for three years. She was married to the silver-haired Per Søderstrom, a distinguished member of one of Stockholm's oldest families who had been a senior lawyer in the Department of Forestry in Stockholm and was the author of *Computational Logic and Crime Detection*. It was thanks to his sophisticated methodology that the police, at last, were making some progress in tracking down Olaf Palme's assassins. Søderstrom was appointed head of a special, top secret unit of *Säpo,* the Security Service of the Swedish police, in charge of anti-terrorist operations, but officially he was given the conventional title of *Kriminalinspektör*, Detective Chief Inspector. It was assumed that a fresh face from outside the service would improve the morale of the Police. There had been more than twenty thousand leads before Per Søderstrom and his computers would make some important breakthroughs.

Amalie had met Søderstrom during a skiing holiday in Saint Moritz, in the winter after her divorce. The world he represented seemed to her to be agreeably mysterious and powerful. He married her for her beauty, her social position, and her money. Relations between him and her three girls, particularly with Ulrike, were excellent. However, after the first few exciting weeks with his new wife, *Kriminalinspektör* Søderstrom decided he preferred computers.

Whenever Amalie and Goethe met, they carried on a mild flirtation. Not for a second did she suspect Goethe's passion for her daughter. He enjoyed playing the part of a gallant, old-fashioned courtier, kissing her outstretched hand when greeting her, while Amalie pretended to be his future lover. They played their respective games to perfection.

Now, in August 1992, she had deliberately chosen the unspectacular Hotel Süss to be near Goethe, though she would have much preferred a larger, more fashionable hotel so that Ulrike could meet eligible young men.

Goethe observed his familiar falling-in-love symptoms with Ulrike with scientific attachment. He became frantic, obsessive, ecstatic. Ulrike may only be nineteen, he said to himself, but she is old enough to help me postpone until further notice my previously scheduled transcendence. He understood that he could not allow himself to die until he had completed *Faust Part Two,* and that to live, he needed a love affair.

On one occasion, when he was alone with Ulrike in the elevator and, before pressing the button, he wanted to make a light-hearted, jovial observation, his brain ceased to function. Without saying a word, she pressed the button for him. In the evening, when recording this incident in his diary, he remarked how delighted he was that she knew his room was on the third floor. He dreamed about her.

In one of his dreams she was climbing a tree. No signal could have been clearer. In the *Elective Affinities* he had drawn analogies between magnetism in love and magnetism in physics. He had not been a friend of one the twentieth century's greatest psychologists, Carl Gustav Jung, for nothing.

———————

"Wolfgang, it's Ulrike."

Ulrike called Goethe from her students' residence in Solnar, a northern suburb of Stockholm. Amalie had encouraged her to move out of the villa in Djurgården, Deer Garden, the fashionable residential area in Skansen, the peninsula just south of the Nobelparken, the Nobel park, so that she could live an independent life among kindred spirits her own age. Mother and daughter were on excellent terms. Ulrike always phoned her mother after she had slept with one of her boyfriends. Amalie invariably approved as long as they took precautions.

It was after dinner. Goethe was in his library, sitting on the Bauhaus armchair Walter Gropius had designed for his father in 1921 in his carpentry workshop in Weimar.

His throat went dry.

"Oh, my dear, how nice of you to phone." He never knew what to call her. His impulse was to say "my child". But he wanted her as woman, not as a child. "Ulrike" was too cold and neutral. "Darling" was impossible. She always turned her head sharply when he tried to speak to her of his love. But she did allow him to hold hands with her when they went for walks together.

"Have you finished your essay?" he asked in his mellifluous Frankfurt baritone.

"I handed it in this morning."

He adored her voice. There was nothing adolescent about it. It was sure of itself and solid. Sometimes he imagined he heard a tinge of Swedish in it, but surely that was only in his imagination since she and her family had lived in Sweden for only three years, although she had spent two of them in a co-educational boarding school near Malmö, to perfect her Swedish. Now she was struggling with Hindu mythology in her Comparative Religion course. How could Goethe help her without pontificating, without condescending?

"Good. Now it's time you threw away your books and got out your skis and drove up to Lapland."

He always told her Nature was a better teacher than all the books in the world, even his own.

"I will, Wolfgang, I will. This time I'm calling because I have something important to say."

Goethe's stomach tightened. The doctor had said "No excitement, please", but surely he could only have meant "No unpleasantness, please." Why would Ulrike phone if she did not have something pleasant to say?

"Wolfgang," Ulrike was untypically excited, joyful, clearly pleased with herself for being able to announce big news. "You've won the Nobel Prize!"

"I thought," he replied with an amused smile in his voice, "you had something important to say." His eyes met those of one of the dozen little Buddhas he had brought back from Burma and placed arbitrarily between books on his shelves.

"Oh Wolfgang, why do you always play games with me? Please be serious, for once. My mother knows somebody in the Academy. It's still a great big secret. How can you say it's not important?"

"Because it isn't for me, my dear. And it shouldn't be for you. They should have given me the Chemistry Prize for my work on world-building microbes. Or the Literature Prize for my *Götz*, when I needed it, in 1946. Or for my *Werther*. Or for my *Egmont*. Or for my *Tasso*. Or for my *Sorcerer's Apprentice* which made Walt Disney rich. But I was never respectable enough for them. They should have paid attention when I published my *Elective Affinities*. But no, the novel was too shocking for them. The world is quite wrong to think that the Swedes are permissive in sexual matters."

Normally, Goethe was too old-fashioned to mention sexual matters in a conversation with a very young girl, especially a very young girl who most probably had never heard of *Elective Affinities*. But she was not just a very young girl – she was Ulrike. He was manic about her, and he had sex on his mind. Never mind that sex had little to do with the Nobel Prize. He rambled on, lecturing her, forgetting that he was telling her things she knew far better than he.

"I know the Swedes talk about sex with less shame and embarrassment than we do, but that doesn't mean very much."

He suddenly remembered a book he had read years ago entitled *The New Totalitarians* by Roland Huntford, who made the point that the only freedom the Swedes took seriously was the freedom to teach sex in school and to encourage the young to experiment freely before marriage – but not after. The Swedes, Huntford wrote, were basically conformist and the concept of individual freedom coming out of the Enlightenment never traveled further north than Denmark. (Didn't Napoleon's Marshal Jean Baptiste Bernadotte, Goethe had wondered when he read the book, bring it with him when he became King Charles XlV of Sweden in 1818?)

"For more than sixty years," he continued, "they've had sex education in the schools. Of course the children have to do a lot of homework for that, and no doubt they have to do exercises and practise what they learn. I'm sure you had to. Right? I've no doubt you've had plenty of sex" – he was going to say "compulsory sex" – "since you were fourteen."

"Fifteen," she corrected him. "Before we moved to Sweden."

Goethe swallowed hard. Oh no! Oh how awful! This will take me a little time to digest. Oh, what disastrous news! It means sex has no more meaning for her than – what? – than irregular verbs? Than ancient Swedish kings? For the moment he merely visualized grim drill masters and drill-mistresses conducting sex classes in gym halls and eventually issuing severe end-of-term reports. "Ingrid's preference for the missionary position shows a serious lack of imagination. Perhaps some outside tutoring will help." Watch it, Wolfgang, he said to himself, no jokes or you'll ruin everything!

"Alright, fifteen," he said bravely. "I'm afraid in my time we had to learn it outside the classroom. No, Ulrike, I was never proper enough for those Nobel Committees of theirs. They didn't like my lifestyle. Of course, I'm going to do the same as my old friend Jean-Paul Sartre, whom I admired so much for a time and who felt acceptance of a Nobel would compromise his independence. I'm not a bit concerned about my independence which, as the world knows, no one can compromise. But I'll say 'no thank you' nevertheless."

"Oh Wolfgang, don't do that."

Goethe's pulse quickened. Why was this so important for her?

"I simply don't have the time for all the fuss. Karl asked me to go to Washington and tell the Senate Committee on Communications what they should do about the new RYH Satellites. I can't let him down."

"But Wolfgang, it's not until December!"

"Never mind, I've other things to do in December. Instead of my coming to Stockholm, why don't you come here?"

"No, no, no, Wolfgang, you must accept."

Ah yes, of course. Her mother put her up to this.

"Look, Ulrike. I'll do anything, anything to be near you. I'll even take out my old skis, give them a good dusting and go to Lapland with you and probably break a leg. But don't you see? I'm too vain to accept the Prize. I refuse to be put in the same category as any common-garden Nobel laureate. After all, don't forget, I am Goethe."

"Oh Wolfgang, I never know when you're serious!"

"I am serious. Only fools are modest, No, my dear. Ask me anything, but please don't ask me to accept the Prize."

Letter from Goethe to Duke Carl August of Saxe-Weimar
Naples, 27–29 May, 1787

*...I heartily approve of the idea of putting Schmidt in
special charge of the finances. He has my full approval and is
in every way the right person. Just one reminder about the
procedure, though. If you make him Vice-President and leave
me more or less at the head, you will make one member of the
Privy Council subordinate to another, which I think it not a
very good idea...*

*I hope to be in Frankfurt at the beginning of September. I
can perhaps stay for a while with my Mother to arrange my last
four volumes, to get my travel notes into better shape, perhaps
to work on my Wilhelm Meister, and at some new ideas...*

*Go on caring for me as you have done in the past and you
will do me more good than I can do myself, than I may hope
and expect. Give me back to myself, to my country, and to
yourself, so that I can begin a new life, and a new life with you.
I lay my whole destiny trustingly into your hand.*

(*Letters from Goethe*, Edinburgh, At the University Press 1957,
#202, page 190.)

———————

*The crescent moon rose above the forest. The warm night lures
Eduard out of the castle. He wanders about. He is the most
restless and the most happy of all mortals. He walks through
the gardens. They are too confining for him. He rushes out into
the fields – they are too large. He is pulled back to the castle and*

finds himself under Ottilie's window. There he sits down, on the steps of the terrace.

"Walls and locks," he says to himself, "separate us. But our hearts are not apart. If she stood in front of me, she would fall into my arms, and I into hers. What else do I need but this certainty?"

(Goethe, *Elective Affinities,* from Chapter 13.)

chapter three

Karl, President and CEO of Saxco, only had two private Gulfstream jets, each with a three-person crew – pilot, flight engineer, flight attendant. As media barons went, he was not in the same league as Bill Gates or Rupert Murdoch, commanders of vast fleets of jets, and he often teased Goethe who, when it suited him, adhered to the small-is-beautiful line. "You have nothing to worry about," Karl said. "After all, you're the star. Not I."

One of the two jets, equipped with an exceptionally good wine cellar, was at this very moment – at ten, Friday, December 4th, 1992 – flying both of them from Frankfurt to Stockholm. Karl's handsome security guard was chatting up the flight attendant while she was preparing the drinks.

Goethe had been right. It was Amalie who had suggested to Ulrike to phone him and inform him ahead of time that the Swedish Academy was about to announce that he won the Literature Prize. That was in October. When Ulrike had reported to her mother what he replied, Amalie spoke to her friends at the Swedish Academy and discreetly arranged a leak to Karl. Amalie correctly guessed that Karl, whom she had seen only on the television news, would insist, for reasons of prestige and publicity, that Goethe accept. She could not know that Goethe had only agreed to go to Stockholm on condition that Karl perform for him a diplomatic mission of the greatest delicacy, involving her.

Amalie wanted very much that Goethe come to Stockholm, to be near him during the Nobel Week, to bathe in his reflected glory and, perhaps, deepen their relationship. Who knows, perhaps he might even ask her to live with him in his palatial villa near Frankfurt. She wouldn't hesitate to leave her husband, because she was getting tired of him. After all, he was only a glorified policeman, however legendary his expertise with computers.

Ulrike, too, wanted Goethe to come. She thought it might be fun to be close to this superstar for a few days, at the very centre of things. Moreover, she did like and admire him. Even at seventy-three, he was an attractive man, definitely *sympatico*. If he wanted to go to bed with her during the festive week, why not? As long as he didn't talk about love. As a matter of fact, it would probably do him good. He had been near death only a few months ago. Better sex than all those doctor's prescriptions.

———————

"You know very well, old man, that I'm entirely at your disposal," Karl had said when Goethe told him he would only accept the Prize if Karl did him a favour in Stockholm. Karl used the phrase *Mein Alter,* meaning literally "old man". "Would you mind being a little more precise?"

"I think I'd rather wait till we're in the air," Goethe had replied.

Now they were in the air. Karl wore a smart skiing outfit, to demonstrate that he was above convention. His oval face, low eyebrows, sharp long nose and prominent pointed chin revealed stubbornness and determination. In small matters like his appearance, Goethe never defied convention. He dressed carefully, with a refined sense of colour. He wore a dark brown sports jacket, black pants, and a striped shirt he had bought in London, with a yellow tie. The flight attendant had taken their fur-lined winter coats to the closet at the front of the plane.

They were flying over the Lahn near Wetzlar. Goethe was looking over the text of his Nobel Lecture he was to deliver on Monday. It was called "The Perfect Moment".

"Well now, Wolfgang. Don't keep me in suspense. What's all this about a 'delicate diplomatic mission'?"

The flight attendant poured wine in their glasses.

"I want you to help me marry a young lady," Goethe announced.

"I must ask them to do something about the noise of the engines. What did you say?"

"You heard me very well, Karl. Let me explain. Do you remember last March when you ordered my obituaries to be ready for your hundred and sixty-nine printing presses in forty-five countries? And to dig up all those ancient film biographies? When the heavenly gates were already half-open to welcome me?"

"I remember. I've been told the Almighty was very disappointed you didn't show up."

"No, Karl. For once you were misinformed. He was not. He insists on my finishing *Faust Part Two* first."

They were now flying over the Harz mountains.

Karl rubbed his chin. He knew Goethe well enough not to ask him what that had to do with getting married.

"Do I know the young lady?"

"You do not. Her name is Ulrike. She's nineteen."

Karl gasped.

"As soon as I'm back, Wolfgang, I'll ask my doctor to take a look at you. I happen to know that he's well acquainted with the early symptoms of Alzheimer's. It'll do wonders for his practice. You'll be his first patient who's just won a Nobel Prize."

"No need to waste his time," Goethe smiled. "My own doctor has already given me the green light. And if the world thinks I have become a little odd in my old age you can quote me and say that it is the errors of a man that make him lovable. That makes me seem suitably modest. But of course I'm not making an error. On the contrary. I'm being entirely reasonable. I need Ulrike. I can't tie her to me through sex because sex means nothing to her. I simply have no choice but to marry her."

They were now over Lübeck, about to cross the Baltic Sea.

"Have you proposed to her?" Karl asked.

"She would say I was out of my mind."

"Clever girl, your Ulrike. Too good for you. So let's talk business. What do you want me to do?"

"It's very simple, Karl. While in Stockholm, I want you to seek a *rapprochement* with Ulrike's mother. As you may remember, I've always felt that it's important to have mothers on one's side. But this time I would like you to assume the burden for me."

Karl remembered Bettina Brentano. Goethe first charmed the

grandmother, then the mother, finally Bettina. The grandmother, fifty years ago, was Sophie La Roche, then came the daughter Maximiliane who was seventeen at the time, and finally, thirty-three years later, Bettina, aged twenty-two.

"I want you to say to the lady," Goethe continued, "that I have confided to you my wish to marry her oldest daughter, Ulrike. This will be a great shock to her. She has unmistakably indicated to me that she wants me herself. Of course she'll get over it in five minutes. She's a very worldly lady. She will decide that if Ulrike marries me she'll be my mother-in-law. You see, all she wants is to be connected with me in some way, to enjoy me, so to speak, vicariously. Once she's calmed down, she'll be perfectly happy. She and Ulrike will have a little talk. She'll say to Ulrike: 'Go ahead, it can't last longer than a year or two. After that you'll be rich and famous as the Great Man's beautiful young widow. You'll be able to pick anyone you choose.' How can any sensible girl say no? Tell the mother, to demonstrate that you're really serious, that if Ulrike accepts me you'll be delighted to establish a trust fund of million marks for each, one million for the mother and another million for the daughter. Then it'll be doubly in the lady's interest that Ulrike says yes. Thanks to Ulrike's abandoned father, they're already very rich, but there's nothing to prevent the very rich from wanting to become even richer. An almost universal phenomenon, as you know very well."

Karl signaled the flight attendant, holding out his glass.

"Wolfgang," he said, "you amaze me."

"I've amazed myself for seventy-three years. And you, Karl, for nearly fifty."

Before they landed on Stockholm's snow-covered Arlanda Airport at noon, Karl had a quick shower in the bathroom and changed into a charcoal-grey suit in the space at the back of the jet which could be curtained off to serve as bedroom during night-flights. By the time they arrived they had finished three bottles of wine between them. It was important to get in the mood. After all, they had been told that, during the Nobel Week, the laureates and their retinues usually began their daily intake of alcohol at breakfast.

––––––

Knut Johannson, the tall and austere Permanent Secretary of the Swedish Academy, who had made the explanatory speech when the

Prize was announced, and the jolly, rotund Baron Gunnar Lennert, the President of the Nobel Foundation, were among forty celebrity-watchers, Saxco officials, TV cameramen, photographers and reporters who greeted Goethe and Karl at the Arlanda airport. It took Goethe a few minutes before he spotted, his barely restored heart beating furiously, Ulrike and Amalie who had stayed discreetly in the background. It was not easy for Goethe to restrain his impatience before being given a chance to allow Ulrike to kiss his forehead, Amalie to hug him, and to introduce both to Karl. First he had to survive the arrival ritual and endure a television interview, while Karl talked to his Saxco people. The Nobel officials told him that the four other laureates and their families, associates and friends had already arrived. They were staying, as he was, in the Grand Hotel. The Nobel Foundation was giving a reception tomorrow afternoon at five, for the laureates and their families and retinues to become acquainted with one another.

Baron Lennert presented Goethe to Karen Svensen, a handsome blonde, blue-eyed lady in her mid-forties, who had been Swedish consul in Milan and who was to serve Goethe as escort, social secretary, transportation and press officer, adviser on matters of protocol, cautioner against slippery floors in banquet halls, and provider of whatever services may help make his stay agreeable. The Ministry of Foreign Affairs made escorts available to all the laureates. The previous year the father of the chemistry laureate bred rabbits, so his escort arranged for him to visit a rabbit farm.

After an exchange of courtesies, Karen Svensen took Goethe to a small television studio, just off the VIP lounge, and introduced him to the interviewer Bengt Nyquist who wore horn-rimmed glasses and a well-worn brown sports jacket, with leather patches at the elbows. He had jotted down the questions he wanted to ask Goethe. Karen Svensen watched the interview through the glass from the control room.

"Herr von Goethe, we're all looking forward to your Nobel Lecture on Monday. I assume you've prepared it."

"I have."

"Since your Nobel was announced in October, there has been a great deal of talk about the New Goethean Age."

"Not by me, sir, I assure you."

Goethe only said "sir" to a person who made no impression on him.

"Nevertheless it is you, your writing, your influence, your example, which has given rise to this idea."

"I do not wish to compare myself to a rose, sir, but I'm sure you realise that when roses are in bloom, they are in bloom everywhere."

Bengt Nyquist took out his handkerchief and wiped his brow. This is going to a tough one, he noted to himself. He looked for the next question on the pad.

"What I wanted to ask you, Herr von Goethe, was whether you can give us some idea what to expect from the twenty-first century."

"Sir, I think the important thing is that we should do the best we can here and now, be as productive and active as possible, and let the future look after itself. But if you really insist on an answer, I would say that I think it's a miracle some of us are still alive, considering our perverse drive to self-destruction. In this century, we've had two world wars costing fifty million dead, many dozens of other wars, several totalitarian monster states, Auschwitz, gulags, Rwanda, AIDS. Still, against all expectations, God has not died. A hundred years ago some of our best thinkers thought that He or She had expired."

"What makes you say this?"

"Because I think a lesson has been learned. That is why I look forward to the next century with some limited, qualified confidence. Too much secularism is lethal. For purely utilitarian reasons, if for no better reasons, many people have learned to accept, willy-nilly, that there's something big and unfathomable out there – and also in here." Goethe vigorously slapped his chest. "That's definitely a step forward. For one thing, they've found out that there's less crime, and less disorder, if religion is held in respect. Even organized religion. I know this is a daring thing to say, for a man who's just arrived in one of the most secular countries in the world."

"Are you yourself a member of a church, Herr von Goethe?"

"I am not. Instead, I'm superstitious. I think superstition is the poetry of life."

Nyquist, quite wrongly, thought this was a joke.

"Leaving utilitarian considerations aside," he went on, "what do you think is the essence of religion?"

"It's the assumption that there's something in us which does not age and which death does not destroy. Let us call it the Factor X. For some, it takes dominance over the body; for others, for the less fortunate ones, the body is in charge. Nature is not democratic or egalitarian. A strong Factor X enables the fortunate, the privileged person possessing it, to lead a good, morally sensitive, productive life, constantly renewing itself, even in old age."

"Admit it, Herr von Goethe, you are describing yourself."

"All I am saying," Goethe went on, ignoring the remark, "is that every creative act of the first order, every significant *aperçu,* every great thought which has great consequences, has a life of its own, a life above the physical. It is a gift from Heaven, and we must receive it with gratitude. By the way, I've always thought ingratitude was a sign of weakness, and I have never known a person of real ability to be ungrateful. Those who are singled out to receive this gift must treasure it and honour it. But they are mere instruments. Shakespeare received the *aperçu* of Hamlet in one moment. He was a mere instrument, a vessel, though evidently the enormous Factor X within him rendered him capable of receiving the gift. To think it through, however, to invent all the characters, the structure, the scenes, the dialogue, requires a productivity of a different, lesser kind – that's hard work."

"You say Nature is not egalitarian?"

"Yes, sir. It has not signed the Bill of Rights."

"I see. I understood you to say that the Factor X is more present in some than in others."

"Obviously."

"It's not just...talent?"

"No, sir." Goethe was becoming restless. "It's something ageless, eternal, within us."

"You mean the soul?"

"No, sir. I do not mean the soul. I mean the spirit within us that's connected to infinity. For many, it's underdeveloped, passive, stifled by the demands of the body. Death overpowers it. But for the happy few it grows organically, according to the laws of Nature, like a tree, renewing itself again and again. To the Factor X in them, death means nothing."

"I assume this will be one of your themes in *Faust Part Two?*"

"Yes, sir. Faust is not Everyman. He is a person of exceptional gifts."

"I see." Nyquist looked at his notes. "Ah yes. This is what I wanted to ask you. Who will win the bet – Faust or Mephisto? Surely you can't send Faust to Heaven, after what he's done to that poor girl. If there's any justice, Mephisto *has* to win his soul."

Goethe shook his head, with mock sadness.

"I'm afraid, sir, I cannot make any promises. You will readily understand that, before I decide how to end the play I will have to consult the Mephisto within me."

With a benign smile and a haughty wave of the hand, Goethe declared the interview terminated.

Karen Svensen took him back to the lounge. By now it was two thirty. The welcoming crowd had dispersed. Ulrike was not to be seen anywhere. But Amalie was there, wearing a beautiful dark blue dress, engaged in animated conversation with Karl. Both were sitting on an armchair, side by side. She had taken off her mink coat and put it on her lap. Very promising, Goethe thought.

When she saw him, she rose, walked quickly towards him and gave him the hug he had expected. Then she shook hands with Karen Svensen. Amalie gave him her daughter's regrets. Ulrike simply did not have to time to wait, she said.

A dark-blue pain seized the lower part of Goethe's abdomen.

———

In December darkness descends on Stockholm at three in the afternoon. When Goethe's limousine arrived it was nearly four. The Grand Hotel stands at the quay of the River Strömmen, between the Opera House and the Dramatic Theatre, and faces the huge, already magnificently lit Royal Palace at the other side of the water.

The corner suite 325 on the third floor facing the Palace was reserved for him. Directly under him, the same size and equipped with the same furniture, was suite 225, reserved for Karl. There were altogether six top-quality suites – for each of the laureates and Karl. A large salon was to serve all of them as hospitality suite.

Goethe opened the curtains as soon as he arrived in his suite, to admire the royal lights. On a glass table there was a bottle of Cognac, a vase of yellow tulips, a bowl of tropical fruit and a little green box from "F. Ahlgrens Tekn. Fabrik AB, purveyors of throat lozenges to Nobel Prize winners since 1909". Also, a red leather case with his program for the week. There was also a thick envelope with the coat of arms of the three crowns of Sweden, containing the invitation to the formal banquet on Thursday in the City Hall, including the guest list, complete with thirteen hundred and eighteen names and titles, their locations at sixty-three tables, and an accompanying diagram. He was seated in the Centre directly opposite the King and next to the Queen. He checked that Ulrike's name was listed among the students at table forty-seven.

In a separate envelope there was the program for the week.

Program

Johann Wolfgang von Goethe

Escort: Mrs. Karen Svensen, Ministry of Foreign Affairs

Friday, December 4th — Arrival, Arlanda Airport

Saturday, December 5th
5:00 p.m. – 7:00 p.m. — *"Get together"* to meet the other laureates and their families
Address: KAK, Bolinderska Festvåningen, Blasiholmshamnen 6

Sunday, December 6th
8:00 p.m. — Visit to Uppsala

Monday, December 7th
10:00 a.m. — *Nobel Lecture*
Johann Wolfgang von Goethe
Swedish Academy
Address: Börshuset — Stock Exchange Building

5:00 p.m. – 7:00 p.m. — *Reception* for laureates and their families given by the Nobel Foundation
Address: Sturegatan 14

Tuesday, December 8th
12:30 p.m. — *Luncheon* given by H. E. the Ambassador of Germany, Herr Dr. Rudolf von Sesenberg, Frau Martha von Sesenberg
Address: Förbundsrepubliken Tysklands, Ambassad, Skarpögatan 0

Wednesday, December 9th
6:00 p.m. — *Reception* given by H. E. the Ambassador of the United States Mr. Leonard Monkland and Mrs. Flora Monkland

Address: American Embassy,
Strandvägen 101

Thursday, December 10th
11:00 a.m   *Rehersal* (for all laureates)
                          Address: Concert Hall, Hötorget

4:00 p.m.   *Prize Presentation* (for 4:30 p.m.)
                          Address: Concert Hall, Hötorget

6:30 p.m.   *Banquet.* White tie and tails
                          Address: City Hall, Blue Hall

Friday, December 11th
10:15 a.m.   *Visit* to the office of the Nobel
                          Foundation in order to collect the
                          Prize money, etc.
                          Address: Sturegatan 14

7:20 p.m.   *Banquet* given by Their Majesties, the
                          King and Queen
                          Address: The Royal Palace

Saturday, December 12th
2:00 p.m. – 4:30 p.m.   *Round Table TV Discussion*
                          "Science and Man"
                          Address: Studio 2, Sveriges Radio/
                          TV, Oxenstiernsgatan 34

Sunday, December 13th
7:00 p.m.   Lucia Dinner
                          Host: Medical Students Association
                          of Stockholm
                          White tie and tails
                          Karolinska Institute
                          Address: Solnavägen 1

Monday, December 14th   *Departure*

He only noticed the scribbled note attached to the vase of yellow tulips after he had read the program and taken off his coat. It was from Ulrike. She had bought the flowers in the lobby ten minutes before Goethe arrived and made sure they would be sent to his room immediately.

He took a deep breath.

Dear Wolfgang,

I hope that you will forgive me for having to leave the airport before your interview was finished. But this is a terrible week for me. I have to hand in three essays. The professors will not accept *any* excuses. This is really bad, after the fuss I made about you having to accept, and all that. But I promise to be at the ceremony. And I already have a ticket for one of those student tables at the banquet in the City Hall.

In the meantime I hope that my mother will look after you a little bit, and that these modest flowers will give you pleasure.

Affectionately,
Your faithful disciple,
Ulrike

A high vaulted Gothic chamber:

Faust: *Look at me. I've worked right through philosophy, right through medicine and jurisprudence, as they call it, and that wretched theology too. Toiled and slaved at it and know no more than when I began.*

(*Faust Part One,* Scene 1. Translation by Barker Fairley, University of Toronto Press 1970, page 8.)

chapter four

On Wednesday, October 14, two days after Ulrike's phone call to Goethe, the Prize-awarding institutions of the Nobel Foundation informed the four other laureates officially by telephone. In Alfred Nobel's testament, Physics came first, Chemistry came second, Physiology or Medicine third, Literature last. The laureates were informed in sequence according to Alfred Nobel's priorities.

1. Physics
Donald Heath, University of Toronto, Canada

From the Citation: "For his investigations of the conditions under which a single stable cavitation bubble can produce sonoluminescence – light from sound."

The Scene: A bedroom in Donald Heath's house, between Avenue Road and Yonge Street, just north of Saint Clair Avenue, in Toronto. The time: A quarter to six in the morning. The lady with him was Catherine. She was not his wife.

"It's for you," Catherine said.

Half asleep, Catherine woke Donald Heath and handed him the phone. The voice sounded urgent. Catherine went back to sleep immediately.

"Professor Heath? O'Brian from the *Toronto Sun*," a hoarse voice said. "What precisely is 'cavitation'?"

Donald Heath, who was wearing striped blue-and-white pyjamas, was known for his reluctance, while awake, to let any occasion go by without light-hearted comment. In his lectures on sonoluminescence he often found the word "cavitation" a rewarding trigger for verbal humour. With his round face, unkempt, curly hair and sparkling eyes, the world-class physicist even looked like a comedian. His reputation must have reached the reporter's ears. On this occasion, however, Heath's impulse was to hang up. But he stopped himself. There was an element in that beery voice that suggested something important.

"Why do you want to know?"

"Because I have to write a story about your Nobel Prize."

"What do you mean?"

"Professor Heath," O'Brian replied, "there's no need to play games with me. Congratulations!"

After allowing a few seconds to let this sink in, Heath poked Catherine. She grunted without opening her eyes. All he could think of was to ask O'Brian why he couldn't have waited a couple of hours before calling.

"Your line would have been busy. By the way, I know perfectly well what cavitation is. We have a dictionary at the *Sun,* you know. I just wanted to get your comments."

"Naturally I'm delighted."

(Cavitation – the rapid formation and collapse of vapour pockets in a flowing liquid in regions of very low pressure. *Random House Dictionary.*)

Catherine rubbed her eyes. She was wearing a pink nightshirt. "What is it, dear?"

Heath whispered the news to her. She nearly choked him with her hug. He rallied and asked O'Brian to excuse him, please.

"Not so quick, Professor Heath. Were you surprised to get the news?"

"It was the last thing I expected. Now goodbye, Mr. O'Brian."

Of course it was a lie that a Nobel was the last thing he expected. Scientists usually know where they stand in the international pecking order. Only last Wednesday he had dreamed that he had won. He had even joked with Catherine about it. It was a sensitive subject because last summer, when she had left her husband, Edward Graziano, professor of genetics at Stanford University in California, to shack up with Donald Heath who had been guest professor there, she had demanded that he had better get a Nobel if he wanted her to stay with him. It was a semi-joke, of course. However, now he met that condition. By pure chance Graziano also won a Nobel this year, for Medicine. This was to have important consequences.

In September, *The Scientist* had named Donald Heath a strong contender on the basis of his publications, the number of times he was cited by his colleagues, his capacity to attract the best people in the field to work with him, and his previous awards. *The Scientist* had discovered that Nobel winners, on average, publish five times more papers and are cited thirty to fifty times more frequently than ordinary scientists.

At the civilized hour of nine o'clock, the Secretary-General of the Royal Swedish Academy of Sciences in Stockholm at last gave him the official news by telephone. Of course Donald Heath pretended that a Nobel was the last thing he had expected.

2. Chemistry
Elizabeth Priestley, Cambridge University, England

From the Citation: "For her discoveries on the catalytic properties of potassium."

The Scene: The High Table in the Great Hall of St. John's College, dominated by the Tudor portrait of Lady Margaret Beaufort, patron saint of the College's Lady Margaret Boat Club, of which Elizabeth was an ardent fan.

Elizabeth was in her early sixties. Her wrinkled face with quick, bright eyes, supported by five layers of double chins, came straight out of Agatha Christie, and her no-nonsense brusqueness was clearly designed to conceal a meltingly soft heart. Few of her clothes were acquired within the last twenty years. She was a life-threatening menace on her bicycle. Her rooms were in the Third Court, with an excellent view of the Bridge of Sighs, designed in 1696 by Christopher Wren. (She and her husband had a big house on Adams Road, not far from the University Library, large enough to contain, if necessary, their four children and eleven grandchildren.) At nine in the morning she was informed of her Prize, at ten she called the girl at the college switchboard and asked her to "pretend to be terribly, terribly pleased and take the numbers."

Elizabeth's pipe-smoking husband, Ramsey Mansbridge, a Fellow of Trinity College next door, was one of the world's most noted paleontologists.

At the High Table, she waved aside all attempts to congratulate her and insisted, following a lovable logic of her own, on reminding everybody that forty years ago she would have "gained blades with three very quick bumps" if she had been allowed to be a member of the Lady Margaret Boat Club. She did not have to explain that at that time there were no women at St. John's.

"What are you going to do with all that money, Elizabeth?" the anthropologist Jeremy Brown asked.

"I'm going to buy myself a new bicycle with twenty-four gears!"

"Oh, may the Lord have mercy on our souls!" a dozen gowned dons exclaimed in unison.

3. Physiology or Medicine
Edward Graziano, Stanford University, Palo Alto, California

From the Citation: "For his discovery of new possibilities in understanding the mutation of rhinoviruses [which cause the common cold] by means of identifying a key protein, using monoclonal antibodies."

The Scene: The library of the Edward Graziano's comfortably furnished, flat-roofed Spanish-style house in Palo Alto, fifty miles south of San Francisco. The geneticist, born in Pittsburgh of Italian parents, was in his early sixties, tall and bald, and universally known for his quick mind, sarcastic tongue, stubbornness, touchiness and infuriating habit of downplaying everything other people think important. Since his wife Catherine, thirty years younger than he, left him the previous summer, there had not been a day without a nasty argument with a colleague, associate or student. Now he was being interviewed by Allison Connor, a respected medical journalist who knew something about the subject and was increasingly impatient with him for refusing to take pride in his achievement. She wore a dark green dress.

"Yes," he said, "it's true that for some time now we've been able to characterize the common cold rhinovirus by X-ray crystallography."

"But now, Professor, you've gone beyond characterization and have achieved the actual identification. Aren't you on your way?"

"On my way to what? No. We've done nothing more than develop a method which opens up new avenues of research. My senior research assistant Dr. Lovett deserves as much credit as I do."

"My dear Professor," Connor shook her head, "the members of the Nobel Assembly at the Karolinska Institute habitually sound out hundreds of scientists in a given field before coming to a decision. They must have considered your achievement an important breakthrough."

"Who knows why they chose me? My guess is they wanted to get away from cancer and AIDS, that's all. Besides, the common cold is a new departure for them. And it will help them win in a popularity contest. Not everybody has cancer or AIDS. Not yet, anyway."

"You're not being fair to yourself, Professor."

"Let me be the judge of that, if you don't mind. I don't think we'll get very far if you start lecturing me."

"I'm sorry, Professor."

Edward Graziano looked at his watch.

"Is it not true," the journalist swallowed hard, "that there are more than a hundred strains of the cold virus, and they're all variants of a few viral types, and most of them mutate constantly?"

"Yes, that's true."

"And is it not also true that most other researchers in the field had given up?"

"You had better ask them, Miss Connor. Now, I'm afraid I have another appointment."

Without further ado, Edward Graziano led his visitor to the door.

4. Literature
Johann Wolfgang von Goethe

The Economic Sciences were not included in Nobel's will. In 1969 the Bank of Sweden filled the gap. It has been awarding an Economic Sciences Prize in Memory of Alfred Nobel every year ever since.

5. The Economic Sciences
Masao Okita, Tokyo

From the Citation: "For his empirically founded interpretation of the considerations which guide trading blocks to engage in free trade or in bargaining-dictated trade."

The Scene: The evening of October 15th, after dinner, during amorous preliminaries with the entertainer Raeka, in her apartment in a small street in the Ginza district in Tokyo. Masao Okita and Tatsuko Shimazu, the Minister of International Trade, jointly paid the astronomical rent of the apartment. Both appreciated her cultivated conversation and refined love-making. According to their free-market principles they did not claim exclusivity on her services.

The telephone rang. Raeka handed Masao the receiver. He

expected it to be his secretary, Tayama, the only person to whom he had given the number, with instructions only to give it to third parties under extreme circumstances. But there had been a hitch in Raeka's electronic control system. The call was for her. Normally she did not take calls while she was entertaining. She excused herself with a polite smile. The call was quite unimportant – a neighbour wanted to borrow a dress.

Masao Okita was a stocky man in his early fifties who wore glasses and parted his black hair in the middle. He had bags under his eye and a bulbous nose with wide nostrils. His public image concealed his kind heart. There were no indications that he was ever concerned with matters other than government finance, banking, the stock market, research, teaching, consulting and investing. No one doubted that he had considerable influence on fiscal and monetary policy, partly thanks to his enormous abilities, partly thanks to his friendship with Tatsuko Shimazu. Of the large sums he gave anonymously to struggling artists, musicians and writers nothing was known publicly. His petite, bird-like, sharp-witted wife Kanya, a professor of anthropology at the University of Kyoto, approved thoroughly, just as she did of his relations with Raeka. These relieved her of the need to share his bed. She had only done so, without enthusiasm, to conceive three children, now in their teens. While he was a practitioner in state-of-the-art global capitalism, she approached her subject in a strictly Marxist perspective.

"What about some country and western?" Masao asked Raeka after she hung up.

"Oh, of course."

Raeka placed a disc in her CD player. She had forgotten that he always found country and western music stimulating.

She slipped her blouse off.

The telephone rang again. This time it was his secretary Tayama. Raeka turned down the music.

"Yes, I understand," he said. "But I don't mind at all if they want to cross-examine me. I think it's better like that. Please call Kishiro, he's got the papers. He'll explain to the committee that I never talked to brokers about it. What? No, I never heard a whisper about kickbacks. That would really surprise me. What I intend to do about Namura is my own affair, I certainly won't discuss it with them. What else did they want to know? Whether my book about Singapore–Indonesian trade has been translated into Portuguese? I've no idea. Better look it up in

the files. Thank you, Tayama. Please try not to call again."
He put the receiver down and undid his belt.
The next call was from Stockholm.

"I swear I've never seen a more beautiful man: forehead, nose and eyes are those of the Olympian Jupiter."

(From a letter of 1829 by Count Wolf Baudisson, quoted in Miszelle: der Grossherzoglich-Weimarische Jupiter, in *Versuche zu Goethe: Festschrift für Erich Heller,* Lothar Striem Verlag, Heidelberg 1976, page 337.)

At last a side door opened and he himself entered. Dressed entirely in black and wearing the star of his order, holding himself almost rigidly erect, he stepped among us like a monarch giving an audience.

(Franz Grillparzer, September-October 1826, quoted in *Goethe: Conversations and Encounters,* edited by David Luke and Robert Pick, Henry Regnery Company, Chicago 1966, page 147.)

chapter five

W hat watches and cheese are to Switzerland, cherry blossoms
to Japan, vodka to Russia, gondolas to Venice, frankfurters
to Frankfurt, baseball to the United States and the RCMP to
Canada, the Nobel Prize is to Sweden.

The Nobel House, the mid-town headquarters of the Nobel
Foundation on Sturegatan 14, is a dignified, five-storied building with
an austere facade. It has the appearance of the private residence of an
unostentatious patrician family. In England the style would be called
Georgian. The building is filled with memorabilia of Alfred Nobel.

In the late afternoon of Saturday, December 5th, 1992, it was the
location of the "get-acquainted reception" hosted by Baron Gunnar
Lennert, President of the Nobel Foundation. Assorted personnel of the
various Nobel institutions, namely the Royal Swedish Academy of
Sciences, the Karolinska Institute and the Swedish Academy, were
present, as well as members of the diplomatic corps and high officials
of the Bank of Sweden. An emissary of the Royal Palace also attended.
In the spirit of the three Scandinavian monarchies, he came by bicycle.

Goethe was amazed at his resilience after Ulrike's rebuff, twenty-
four hours before this reception. These sudden swings in his mood
were characteristic of the state of which Klärchen sings in *Egmont:*

Sky-high exulting,
Despairing to death.

By now he had regained his balance; he was neither one nor the
other, partly because he knew that Karl and Amalie were getting on
well. Today they had lunch together and were meeting again for

dinner. This, he hoped, augured well for the success of Karl's diplomatic mission. He happily left them alone, rather than insisting on their accompanying him to the reception. Karen Svensen was more than capable of looking after him. She agreed there was no need to arrive punctually at five. Six o'clock was good enough.

This gave Donald Heath enough time to discuss skiing in Banff with the skinny wife of Baron Gunnar Lennert, before Goethe's arrival when inevitably all normal conversation would stop. Elizabeth Priestley could tell a polite man from the Swedish Academy that she had forgotten the script of her Nobel Lecture and was having it faxed to the hotel while her husband, the paleontologist Ramsey Mansbridge, was able to inform the French Ambassador that dinosaurs were by no means extinct but had simply evolved into birds. Edward Graziano could still learn from a talkative surgeon on the staff of the Karolinska Hospital that lawyers would soon be allowed to plead bad genes as a defence to every crime under the sun, even though Graziano's mind seemed to be on other things and he didn't say a word. "Goodbye free will," the surgeon said, laughing, "goodbye personal responsibility!" The amiable Robert Lovett, Graziano's senior research assistant to whom he had given generous credit in his interview with the medical reporter, had time to chat with Masao Okita about Japanese-owned asparagus fields in northern California. Okita's command of English was excellent, except that, like many Japanese, he had occasional difficulties with prepositions. He said, referring to the cost of irrigation, "About that I have nothing to add." And his wife Kanya Okita still had time to give Baron Lennert a lecture on the extraordinary success of prison reform in Castro's Cuba.

There was a hush when Goethe entered the room, accompanied by Karen Svensen. He was impeccably dressed in a dark blue suit and a dotted light blue tie, a pink rose in his buttonhole. On his face there was a faint hint of a benign smile. No one in the room, other than those few who had met him the day before at the airport, had ever seen Goethe in the flesh. This was one of the great moments in their lives, the entrance of the man who was to give the new era the label the "Goethean age". The four other laureates most certainly could not compete with that. Donald Heath and Elizabeth Priestley conveniently forgot that they had publicly questioned Goethe's findings on environmental geobiology. And Ramsey Mansbridge wished he had never caused sympathetic laughter at the Trinity High Table in Cambridge when he mockingly asked when at last Goethe's DNA

Odes and Sulphuric Acid Elegies were going to hit the bookstands.

This moment could only be compared to the Pope arriving in the lounge of the Nobel Foundation on Sturegatan 14, which he had never done, and holding out his hand to have the Ring of Saint Peter kissed. It was regrettable that Goethe had no title which would justify a Your Holiness, a Your Majesty, Your Grace, Your Highness or even Your Excellency. Otherwise Baron Lennert would have been able to do a lot better than the embarrassingly inadequate "Herr von Goethe" with which he introduce him to the assembled guests.

"You're very kind, Baron." Goethe helped himself to a glass of white wine. "It is most enjoyable to be in such distinguished company, among so many eminent and generous people." His mellifluous baritone never sounded better.

The Baron took Goethe by the arm and shepherded him in the direction of the laureate in chemistry, Elizabeth Priestley.

"I hope you put your lecture in your suitcase, Goethe," she said after some preliminary small talk. "I forgot mine. Isn't that awful? Oh, you've probably memorized yours."

"By no means, *madame.*" What was he to call this eccentric old professor? "I have a good memory only for things that rhyme. I'm afraid my paper is very prosaic."

"Does it have a name?"

"The Perfect Moment."

"A perfect moment for me to butt in," the brash Canadian physicist Donald Heath said. His hair was more than usually unkempt and he was feeling no pain. "I've been waiting to tell you for years what *The Sorcerer's Apprentice* is actually about."

Goethe looked at him with his famous dark-brown, lustrous, luminous, translucent eyes.

"Yes?"

"It's about Man and all the latest computer gadgets we can't seem to do without. They're taking over the world. Please stop it."

"I've forgotten the formula," Goethe smiled.

"Oh no!" Heath exclaimed. "Now we're doomed."

A minute later is was Masao Okita's turn to interrupt. Aquavit accentuated the bags under his eyes.

"Did I hear the word 'doom'?" he asked. "For years I've been trying to translate it for Japanese." He was having his usual trouble with prepositions. "'Doom and Gloom' is a specialty of the West. That's why we Japanese love your *Faust* so much, Professor Goethe. As you know with your royalties – I mean from your royalties – it's always sold out in Japan. We understand it. It's about success. What you call striving. Striving for success. There's no doom in *Faust*."

"Not yet," Goethe observed.

"Don't tell me my wife is right," Masao cried, aghast. "I'd forgotten she warned me there was more to come." He lowered his voice and whispered in Goethe's ear. "She hopes in the end your Faust will proclaim the *Dictatorship of the Proletariat.*"

"She may be right," Goethe replied solemnly. "I still haven't decided."

———

There was a private dining room and a bar in the penthouse on top of the Saxco Tower, a certain distance south of the "Bunker", the secluded, heavily guarded, top-secret headquarters of the special *Säpo* unit headed by Amalie's silver-haired husband, *Kriminalinspektör* Per Søderstrom. The location of the Saxco Tower was far from secret. On the contrary, it could clearly be seen by the King and Queen in their snow-covered Royal Palace.

After drinks in the bar they went to the dining room. A white-jacketed waiter was waiting for them.

Karl and Amalie studied the menu.

Amalie chose a green salad with truffles, poached salmon, and *kaldomar* (stuffed cabbage) with lingonberries, Karl decided on lobster and a steak, rare. He poured the wine.

"Goethe's now been a widower for seven years," Amalie said during the main course. I don't think his wife was much fun for him in her last years, during the day, or the night. Too much drinking. He needs me. I'm exactly the right person for him. He needs care, and attention, and organization, and just a little bit of sex. He needs it to do his work, which is the important thing. But the conditions have to be right. What do you think?"

By now the waiter was serving the first course.

"I think, Amalie. You're making a very powerful case. But I also need care, attention, organization, and quite a lot sex. Why doesn't anybody ever think of me?"

"Oh, forgive me," she laughed, putting her hand across the table, to squeeze his. "I thought that was understood. You're certainly going to get the sex. I'm not so sure about the other things."

"Well, good, thank you," he said. "Now, you asked what do I think about your coming down to Oberreifenberg, to sweeten his remaining years?"

"Yes, that's what I asked."

"Nothing is impossible," Karl looked at his fingernails. "But I think it would take great skill to arrange. His son, August, and August's wife, Ottilie, would certainly object vehemently. They would regard you as a lethal danger to them. One would have to work out a Napoleonic strategy."

"You don't need Napoleon. It's very simple. Because I wouldn't be a danger to them at all. I wouldn't expect to inherit anything. I don't need it."

It was time for the next course, and for more wine.

"I suppose one could make that clear," Karl remarked thoughtfully. "And I could find them another house."

By the time they had coffee and cognac, Karl came to the point.

"Eureka, I've got it!" he cried. "I think I can persuade the old man," he said. "Ulrike!"

Amalie frowned.

"What about Ulrike? What's she got to do with it?"

"Goethe told me he was impressed by Ulrike," Karl said. "You should send her down for a few weeks, to get him used to having a member of your family near him."

Amalie sipped her cognac.

"You can take her into your confidence," he went on. "Tell her she should prepare the ground for you, so to speak."

Amalie thought it over.

"Yes, I can see that. We're on very good terms, of course, and I'm sure she'll always try to help me out if I ask her for something important. But why should she do it? It would be very selfish of me to ask her. She's in the middle of term."

"Oh that," Karl waved it aside with a generous gesture of his right arm. "I can easily arrange that. That's nothing. My people can talk to both universities, in Stockholm and Frankfurt, and we'll have her transferred in no time. She wouldn't lose a thing. And she can easily commute to Frankfurt from Oberreifenberg. A lot of kids do it. It would be a tremendous opportunity for her. How old is she? Nineteen? Just right! Imagine what it would do for her career, whatever she chooses to do, to have spent a little time with Goethe. And then, when the time is up, you move in and take over. What about it?"

There was no need to discuss the matter further later during the pillow talk in the executive bedroom on the fifteenth floor of the Saxco Tower.

O'er all the hill-tops
Is quiet now,
In all the tree-tops
Hearest thou
Hardly a breath;
The birds are asleep in the trees:
Wait, soon like these
Thou, too, shall rest.

(Translated by H. W. Longfellow, from Goethe's *Selected Poems*, edited by Christopher Middleton, John Calder, London 1983, page 58.)

Through   practice, teaching, reflection, success, failure,
furtherance and resistance, and again and again reflection,
man's organs unconsciously and in free activity link what he
acquires with his innate gifts, so that a unity results which
leaves the world amazed.

(Goethe's last letter, written on March 17th 1832, five days before his death, to Wilhelm von Humboldt. *Letters from Goethe*, Edinburgh, at the University Press 1957, page 537.)

Lynceus the Watchman, singing on the battlements:

Born with these eyes, appointed to watch, pledged to the tower,

I like the world. I look at the distant, I look at the near. I see the moon and stars, see forest and stag. And enduring beauty in everything. Content with it all, I'm at ease with myself. You happy eyes, when all is said. Whatever you saw, it was lovely to see.

(*Faust Part Two*, Scene 47, translation by Barker Fairley, University of Toronto Press 1970, page 192.)

chapter six

Excerpts from Goethe's Nobel Lecture,
Monday, December 7th, 1992

The Perfect Moment

It seems that Mozart was a stunning improviser at the piano. Of course he also had an impeccable musical memory. But if we had asked him to repeat a passage he would not have been able to do it, not with any precision. No brain is a recording machine. No brain can stand still. No brain is a computer.

Brain researchers study the connections within neuronal groups which process the individual's experiences and perceptions, revising and reorganizing them constantly. Moreover, going beyond the individual, in order to understand how the mind works the evolutionary psychologists are now asking Darwinian questions to see how the mind has adapted over time to cope with ever-changing challenges. Devising strategies to pass human genes from one generation to the next alone had absorbed a good deal of the mind's time and energy. As the Lord says in the Prologue in Heaven in my *Faust Part One,* "Striving and erring, you can't have one without the other." Striving and erring – in other words: Evolution.

———

While we're alive we progress and we regress. A plant reaches a perfect moment, the climax of bloom. But what about us? Even in the womb we're restless. In *Faust,* I don't know who's more restless – Faust or Mephisto. They compete in restlessness. Right at the beginning of the poem, when the Lord assigns Mephisto to serve as traveling companion to Faust, he sets the mood by telling him that He had never hated his sort. "Of all the negative spirits," the Lord said, "your roguish kind gives me the least concern. It's so easy for men to slump and before long they want to do nothing at all." In short, the Lord engaged the Devil to prevent men from slumping, from doing nothing at all. He wants men to be restless, to be active. No wonder restlessness lies at the centre of their wager. If Faust rests for one perfect moment and exclaims "Oh, this is so beautiful! Let me linger! I want this moment to last for ever!" Mephisto wins and he's lost everything. Rest is a state of harmony between man's inner and his outer reality. That is the rest which Mephisto will not allow Faust and which Faust is prepared to surrender in return for excitement and experience. One would have thought that it was in Mephisto's interest to lay a few traps and trick him into having a perfect moment. But such a device never occurs to him. He knows his main job is to keep Faust on the move, rather than to destroy him. Furthermore, it would have been out of character for either party – and out of character for me who hates pedants – to take the wager very seriously. Poets are rarely consistent. When Faust ecstatically makes love to Gretchen, Mephisto never interrupts to say, "Watch it, my boy. You're approaching a perfect moment!" And in *Part Two* I intend to give Faust at least one night of love with Helena, on stage or off. I will most certainly make sure that Mephisto stays safely out of the way.

———

There was one occasion, when I myself had an extraordinary experience of peace, calm and rest and it became important in my career as a writer. On September 6, 1950, I climbed up to the top of the Feldberg, the highest mountain in the Taunus, very close to the place where I now live. It's a pleasant, well-marked, upward walk, not too steep, through the forest. It takes only about two hours. There's a radio tower on top which was used for air defence during the war, and a restaurant. But there's also a little inn, with a few rooms to rent, where I occasionally spent a night. On that memorable day, in September

1950, I watched the sunset and then wrote a short little poem on the wall of my room, with my fountain pen. I know it's a strange thing to do but I told the innkeeper about it afterwards. We knew each other. He laughed and said he would keep it there, and charge double for the room. The poem became known as the *Wanderer's Nightsong*. As a matter of fact, I wrote two poems, but this one became the famous one. It's still there, I suppose you can see it, any time. The place has changed hands several times since 1950. I don't know whether they charge double, or triple, now. I suppose I should find out, since it's so close to home.

I say "I wrote it", and I can't deny that I did, but it seems to have been written by angels who were probably singing at the same time, too, but I couldn't hear them. This little poem became very, very famous, thanks to the professors who say it's the most flawless poem in the German language. It's the poem about the little birds being silent in the forest. It is the poem many of you probably know. It's so famous that poor innocent children have to learn it by heart. Fortunately for them, it's very short. About four dozen composers have set it to music, so far. A Indonesian airline tried to set it to rock music, for a television commercial, but my lawyers managed to stop them.

Writing the poem was, for me, nearly a perfect moment. I was alone *in* Nature. I experienced a sense of unity *with* Nature. I was *part* of Nature. I became, so to speak, for a nearly perfect moment, Nature itself. I was allowed to forget the painful truth about human existence – that it is separate from Nature, that it is individualized, not universal, that it is essentially ambivalent, part spirit, part nature, part striving for sensation, part striving for rest, for peace. I became one with the little birds who were silent in the forest, by no means out of consideration for me but because they're usually silent in the middle of the night. They need their sleep. I was also one with my beloved microbes who were busy-busy-busy under the solid rocks of the Feldberg. Unlike the little birds, they don't need any sleep at all.

I said it was nearly a perfect moment. My last two lines were, in so many words, "Wait, soon, like the little birds, thou, too, shall rest." I was being a poet, not a prophet. I must have known that I was being ambiguous. On the one hand, I may have been anticipating a perfect moment of rest, after a particularly exhausting time in my life. On the other hand, I may also have been thinking of eternal rest, though I was just over thirty, in excellent health, and in love. As a matter of fact, I had been to that very spot before, with the woman I loved, and I phoned her immediately after I finished the poem. My mind was on love, not on death.

In any case, I have never believed that thinking dark, somber thoughts was very good for the human spirit, under any circumstances. The line sounded right. Let others decide what I meant. Perhaps the poem became so famous because, to this day, nobody has been able to figure it out.

————

It was no accident that I only anticipated a perfect moment, on that memorable occasion on top of the Feldberg, rather than experiencing one. I already sensed something which I now understand much better. One can never have a perfect moment. As my friend Friedrich Schiller used to say, none of us ever experience pure, untempered, unadulterated joy. One can achieve happiness only in activity, not in rest. I discovered it in Burma, soon after that experience on the Feldberg, where I achieved great happiness by being extremely busy, exploring, studying, writing, talking. I firmly believe it now. Of course one needs periods of rest, one needs changes of scene, one needs relaxation, refreshment, renewal, rejuvenation, change. Still, to achieve happiness one has to be active. One has to be restless. Happiness, in the pedestrian language of social scientists, is *process*. This is not only Faustian; it is human and has nothing to do with the work ethic. I would never presume to preach to people about the blessings of hard work, and I would deeply resent anyone preaching to me on the subject. No, it's an observation I've made in myself and in others. I don't think work – by that I mean being voluntarily active and preferably doing productive work – is a duty. It is not demanded by any ethical code. No, it is an aspect of the Nature of Man. If people want to be happy, they work, whether for money or for pleasure, not to seek an illusory perfect moment, but to achieve satisfaction in life, in short to be happy.

This insight has intriguing political implications. The question may be asked whether societies have perfect moments, either in the past, in the present or in the future? This is a question which divides the Left from the Right. The Left tends to believe that, at least in theory, such a moment is attainable, while the Right doubts it. I've always been uncomfortable with labels, but I must confess that I tend to agree with the Right about this, but only because I am opposed to having illusions.

I know we all have them, but, as a practical person, I think they should be reduced to a minimum. In their approach to most day-to-day questions I usually support the Left, and, whenever I have the choice, the Green Parties.

Let me return to the subject of individual happiness. Why, you may ask, do so many writers – I mean, of course, writers other than myself – prefer writing about unhappiness to writing about happiness? Why do so many writers love suffering, perversity, sordid crime, disease and disaster? The answer is because they think that only stupid people are happy, that happy people are trivial, shallow and smug. Happiness, to them, is uninteresting, a subject unworthy of them.

Even one of the writers I revere most, Leo Tolstoy, opened his Anna Karenina with the idea that all happy families are alike, but every unhappy family is unhappy in its own way. We all strive and err. When Tolstoy wrote that sentence, he erred. There is not a single error I cannot imagine committing myself, so I forgive him. A writer who rendered happiness as splendidly as Tolstoy was entitled to err occasionally.

The Swedish Academy, however, took a less indulgent view. It gave the Nobel Prize to me and not to him.

No peace of mind
Heartache and pain
No peace I find
Ever again.

Gretchen at the Spinning Wheel.
Urfaust.

(Goethe's *Selected Poems,* edited by Christopher Middleton, John Calder, London 1983, page 37.)

chapter seven

For nearly a week, from Friday, December 4th, when he caught a glimpse of her at the Arlanda Airport, to Thursday, December 10th, the day of the Prize presentation, Goethe did not see Ulrike. The only communication that took place between them during the week was the gift of yellow tulips, with the accompanying note. How much he would have liked her to come with him on Sunday to visit the University of Uppsala, where he knew a number of professors. Instead, he stayed in Stockholm and worked on his lecture. He knew that Karl and Amalie were seeing each other, but for fear of getting a negative answer he did not ask Karl directly whether he'd had a chance to explore the situation with Amalie.

Goethe met Amalie at the luncheon at the German embassy on Tuesday and, of course, said nothing about Ulrike. As usual, he kissed her hand and played the elderly courtier while she was more flirtatious than ever. He thought she was making a special effort to show her affection, but perhaps he was imagining it. If true, he wondered what it meant.

Behind his back, mother and daughter had spoken twice during the last two days.

"What are you going to wear at the ceremony on Thursday?" Amalie asked Ulrike on the telephone on Sunday evening. Ulrike was in the students' residence in Solnar and was writing an essay about Pythagoras.

"Frankly, Mother, I haven't given it a moment's thought."

"Well, in that case I suggest we meet tomorrow at four o'clock at

Madame in the *Biblioteksgatan* and I'll buy you a dress."

Ulrike reluctantly accepted.

"Well, now," Amalie said, the next afternoon, while the saleslady was wrapping a light blue evening dress they had agreed on. "I have something to ask you. Did you know that Goethe is very impressed by you?"

"As a matter of fact, I did," Ulrike said. "Why do you ask?"

"Because it's been suggested that you switch universities for a semester or two, and spend a little time in his proximity, as his guest. It would do him good. You know, he was very ill last winter. He still hasn't fully recovered."

"Hm...What do you mean 'It's been suggested'? Did he suggest it?"

"No, his friend Karl did. Goethe himself knows nothing about it. What do you think? I don't want to talk you into it."

"I don't think it's out of the question," Ulrike replied thoughtfully. "I've always admired him. And I'm pleased he likes me. I feel badly that I've hardly seen him this week. I'm sure he's annoyed with me. Besides, whatever I do later, a little time with him and his bosom-buddy Karl might be useful. Let me think about it. When do you need an answer?"

"The sooner the better."

Early Wednesday evening Ulrike phoned her mother. Amalie was having dinner with Karl. Ulrike left a message with her answering service simply saying "Why not?" Then it occurred to her that, under the circumstances, it might be a good idea to call Goethe directly. Of course she would not refer to what her mother had told her.

When Goethe arrived back at the hotel from the reception at the American embassy he found the message.

His heart pounded as he dialed her number.

"Oh hello, Wolfgang. I hear your lecture was a huge success."

Goethe swallowed hard.

"Thank you, my dear."

A wave of gratitude to Fate swept over him for having sent him so late in life this marvellous girl whose idealism and ambition had kept him entranced for so many months.

"I'm sorry I had to miss it. But I'm having terrible problems with my essays."

"I don't know why you don't let me write them for you."

"I wish I could," Ulrike said with a sigh. "I'm sorry but I really do have to do the work myself. I know you don't believe in work. You want me to go to Lapland to ski."

"That's right." Goethe smiled as he remembered what he had said to her, way back in October. "What about you and me going off together, after all this is over? Wouldn't a little fresh air do us a world of good?"

"What a good idea," Ulrike said, not very convincingly. "I think I could borrow a pair of skis for you." She changed her tone. "So tomorrow is the big day."

"Yes, Ulrike," Goethe said sadly. "It's you who got me into this."

"I know, Wolfgang. Should I say I'm sorry?"

"I won't be able to answer that until I'm on the plane flying home. Will I see you tomorrow?"

"Yes, Wolfgang. This time I won't let you down. I promise I'll be there."

Yes, I feel it — I know I can believe what my heart tells me —
how can I pronounce these heavenly words — she loves me?

(Goethe, *The Sorrows of Young Werther*, Diary entry for July 13th.)

———

[Speaking of the commedia del arte in Naples] One of
Pulcinello's most effective comic devices on stage was that
occasionally he was not embarrassed to interrupt the action
and yield to the call of nature. "But my dear husband," his wife
then called to him, "you seem to forget where you are, that there
are many people watching you." "E vero, e vero," Pulcinello
replied among great applause.

(J. P. Eckermann, *Gespräche mit Goethe*, F. A. Brockhaus,
Wiesbaden 1959, February 14, 1830, page 544.)

———

Through nothing do people reveal their characters more than by
what they laugh about.

(Maxim 12. Goethes Werke, Kleine Ausgabe, *Maxime und*
Reflektionen, Bibliographisches Institut, Leipzig.)

chapter eight

E very year the ceremony takes place on December 10th, the anniversary of Alfred Nobel's death in 1896, since 1926 in the Concert Hall on the Hötorget, the Haymarket. The facade of Corinthian columns and the Orfeus fountain by Carl Milles in front are among Stockholm's most famous sights. In the summer there is an open-air flower market on the square, just south of the P.U.B. department store where Greta Gustafsson sold hats before she became Greta Garbo.

Goethe deliberately took it easy in the morning to save his energy for his forthcoming television appearance before a world audience. While he was having a leisurely breakfast in his room reading *Le Monde*, Karl dropped in to tell him that he was making excellent progress in the performance of his diplomatic mission. Amalie had spoken to her daughter. Ulrike had agreed to switch universities from Stockholm to Frankfurt for a semester or two and spend a few months in Oberreifenberg as his guest. Nothing had been said so far about marriage. But surely this was a promising first step. However, it would not be a good idea for him to say anything about it directly to Ulrike at this stage. Let her broach the subject.

Goethe was in excellent spirits when he and Karl arrived in the Nobel Foundation's pearl-grey Volvo stretch-limousine for the rehearsal at the Concert Hall at eleven. Karen Svensen had pointed out to him that it was not a dress rehearsal. In the past some American laureates had even worn T-shirts, she said. Accordingly, Goethe wore his maroon turtleneck sweater and grey slacks, and Karl a jogging outfit, under their fur-lined winter coats.

The purpose of the rehearsal was, among other things, to teach republican laureates how to behave with Royalty.

The stage was dominated by the bronze plaque of Alfred Nobel and the floor was covered by a blue carpet with the three crowns of the coat of arms of Sweden. Arrangements of white chrysanthemums and ferns decorated the stage. Two semi-circles of chairs on either side of the speaker's lectern were intended for the laureates on the left and the officials of the award-giving institutions on the right.

Student leaders in yellow and blue uniforms acting as marshals – *marskalker* – welcomed the laureates and their companions, helped them out of their overcoats and guided them to their seats in the front row of the empty auditorium.

Edward Graziano, however, refused all offers of assistance and kept his black overcoat on. Unlike the others, he sat at the back of the auditorium. He arrived alone, without an escort, probably by taxi. He had not shaved and wore an ordinary dark suit and an open shirt. What an unprepossessing man, Goethe thought once again. They had met at the various events during the last few days. Each time Goethe was repelled by Graziano's misanthropy and lack of social graces. Graziano's handsome researcher Robert Lovett arrived five minutes later and sat down with him, accompanied by a lovely girl of about thirteen, blonde, blue-eyed and pubescent, or, as Goethe sometimes put it, "visibly undergoing her first puberty". He had recently observed that particularly gifted persons often had more than one puberty. Of course, he was thinking of his own passion for Ulrike.

Whether this girl was a particularly gifted person, he could not tell. In any case, she came straight from a Swedish film version of *Lolita*. She's probably doing well in her beginners' sex class, Goethe thought. With luck and enough practice, one day, she would no doubt graduate *summa cum laude*. Who was she? The daughter of a Swedish friend? Goethe made a mental note to find out from Graziano or Lovett at the earliest opportunity. Once he finally managed to take her eyes off her, he saw Lovett hand Graziano an envelope. Graziano tore it open impatiently, glanced at the letter, got up furiously and sat down a few rows nearer the stage. Goethe wondered what was going on, then turned around several times to catch Graziano's eye, but without success.

Once Goethe was on the stage, he exuded radiance. On public occasions he often wore his stiff, glum and unsmiling *Mumiengesicht* –

the expression he copied from the faces of five thousand year old mummies in the museum in Cairo – to make people keep their distance. But on this occasion, in view of the splendid news about Ulrike which Karl had conveyed, he was all smiles. Soon, he was sure, he would be ready to tackle *Faust Part Two*. The economist Masao Okita, with his sad bags under his eyes, sat down next to him. His left-wing, bird-like wife joined him on the other side. Karen Svensen, looking very smart in an elegant beige tweed suit, was making polite conversation with the paleontologist Ramsey Mansbridge, while his wife Elizabeth Priestley took a swig of whiskey from the bottle that the physicist Donald Heath had brought along in his hip pocket, an ancient and honourable Canadian custom, he explained to one and all. Karl was interested in the television arrangements and was cross-examining the director in the control room to the right of the balcony.

Baron Gunnar Lennert, the rotund and jovial President of the Nobel Foundation, in shirt sleeves, suddenly appeared from the wings, stepped on the stage and demanded attention. Acting as master of ceremonies, he welcomed his guests and declared that "this was going to be painless" and would not take very long.

"All you have to do this afternoon," he went on, "is listen to the music. While you're still having drinks off stage, you will hear a rousing trumpet flourish. That is meant for you. So you quickly gulp down your drink and get ready for the procession. The orchestra will play the *Trumpet Voluntary* by Jeremiah Clarke. That's an old tradition. You will walk into the Hall at the head of the procession. Everyone will rise. This will be the first, and probably the only time in your lives when you take precedence over Royalty. *You* are the Kings and Queens, so to speak, for the day. The other, far less important King and Queen and members of their family will walk in in your shadow, at the tail end of the procession. Each one of you will be conducted by the member of your respective committee who will later introduce you to the audience. I shall call them the 'introducers'. You will sit down over there" – he pointed to the five chairs to the right of the lectern – "Physics first, Chemistry second, Medicine third, Literature fourth. This was the order in which Alfred Nobel listed his Prizes in his will. Since he omitted to list Economics, the Bank of Sweden's generously endowed the Economic Sciences Prize in Memory of Alfred Nobel in 1969. The fifth chair, therefore, was for the Economics laureate. The introducers and I will sit down opposite you. Behind us on the stage there will be many rows of dignitaries, including a few former laureates who can't stay away from Nobel Prize ceremonies and who will have walked in with you. King Carl Gustav and Queen Silvia will sit down on these gilded chairs." He pointed to them, quite near to where they were sitting. "The orchestra will play the King's Song. Everybody will join in:

"From the heart of the Swedish people
We sing a simple song to the King.
Be faithful to him
And to his family
Make the crown on his head easy to carry.
Believe in him, Swedish people!

"After singing the King's Song we will all sit down. Then I have to make an opening address. I warn you now, it will be interminable. After that, at last, the ceremony proper begins. For each of you, members of the Stockholm Philharmonic Orchestra, strategically placed on the balcony up there, will play the short piece that has been chosen. The printed musical program is distributed at the door. For each of you there will be a separate trumpet flourish, intended to wake you up. The introducer will make a speech about your achievement. It will be too late for you to suffer sudden spasms of modesty, or to challenge the facts. You step down these steps — careful, don't fall! — and he will introduce you to His Majesty. You exchange a few, I hope polite, words with him. You will be presented with your gold medal in a red box and your diploma, each one of course specially designed, and each one in a red leather folder. There will be applause. You bow to the audience, right, left and centre. In a moment I will go through all the steps with you. By the way, please be sure not to lose your gold medals. Three or four years ago — we were still in the middle of the Cold War — two of our Prize winners got them mixed up. One went to New York, the other to Siberia. It took a year of delicate diplomatic negotiations to straighten things out.

"All right, let's go. If you don't mind, I'll pretend to be the King. In the meantime, do you have any questions?"

Elizabeth Priestley instantly raised her hand.

"My dear Baron, I most certainly have. When do we get our money?"

"You have not read the program, Professor Priestley," Baron Lennert replied after the laughter had died down. "You deserve a serious rebuke. If you had read it you would know that you are invited to the Nobel House to tomorrow morning to pick up your cheque. I suggest you take great care with it. Deposit it immediately in a bank account, or at the hotel. A couple of years ago Swedish television carried a very exciting crime story about the theft of the Nobel money. I pray that nothing happens this year that might be the subject of a crime story."

Donald Heath had another question. He delivered it with the timing of an experienced television comedian.

"Do we have to speak to His Majesty in Swedish?"

"An excellent question, Professor Heath. No, you do not. He speaks very good English. For that matter, most Swedes do – we have to begin learning it as a second language in elementary school. But of course you knew this very well and you're just pulling my leg. Your reputation as a chronic leg-puller has preceded you. I assume what you really mean is – in what language will we conduct the proceedings? Am I right?"

"Exactly."

"Well, as a matter of fact, in Swedish. But all our speeches are carefully prepared beforehand and translated. You will be given little booklets with the translations when you arrive this afternoon. Any other questions?"

Masao Okita felt acute pressure to compete for laughs with the Canadian physicist.

"Yes, Baron. I do have a question. I have examined the last Annual Report of the Nobel Foundation from – I mean with – the greatest care and discovered serious flaws in your fixed-interest investments. Especially in the area of convertible debentures. Are you sure there's enough money in the kitty for us?"

"Good question!" cried Elizabeth Priestley.

"If the cheques bounce," replied the Baron, deadpan, "you may sue me. Herr von Goethe," he looked straight at him, "you have been strangely silent. Could it be that you don't approve of the music our Committee has chosen for you?"

Goethe looked at the program and smiled.

"May I say what it is?" the Baron asked.

"Please do."

"It is the theme from the great Faust–Gretchen love duet from the rock version of the first part of *Faust.*"

Someone at the back of the hall, probably one of the *marskalker,* began whistling the tune, and everybody laughed.

"And when you come this afternoon," the Baron concluded the rehearsal, "don't forget to bring your identification papers. You know what police are like. Your white tie and tails won't be enough to identify you. Any terrorist can wear a white tie and tails."

"This occupation with the ideas of immortality," he continued, "is for people of rank, and especially for ladies who have nothing to do. But an able person who wants to amount to something and who therefore has to strive every day, to struggle and to produce, leaves the future world to look after itself itself, and is active and useful in this one."

(J. P. Eckermann, Gespräche mit Goethe, F. A. Brockhaus, Wiesbaden 1959, *Conversations with Eckermann*, February 24, 1824, page 72.)

---

chapter nine

B y the time they emerged from the Concert Hall it was snowing heavily. The limousine was waiting near the Orfeus Fountain. The driver opened the door. This time Karl preferred to take Saxco's Mercedes.

Suddenly, before Goethe and Karen Svensen could step into the limousine, Graziano appeared from nowhere and blocked their path.

"Just a moment, please," Karen Svensen intervened. "We have little time to waste. We've got to get back to the hotel to change. So, if you don't mind..."

"I have no time to waste at all," Graziano insisted. "I must speak to Goethe."

Goethe put on his *Mumiengesicht.*

"Come with me in my cab, Goethe." Graziano's voice was hoarse with urgency. "I know this is a breach of all the rules. But I must speak to you at once. Alone."

Goethe stared at him. Let me see, he thought, not without inner amusement, how I am going to handle this?

"You are the medical man, not I," Goethe remarked serenely. "I'm not a doctor. Nor a psychiatrist. Nor a father confessor."

"You are Goethe," Graziano said. "I need you. Come!"

"I'll see you at the hotel in a few minutes," he said to Karen Svensen. Graziano followed him into the cab.

"I heard your lecture on Monday." The driver shut the glass partition behind him and turned on the ignition. "Most of it seemed pretty obvious to me. But now I know for sure you're the man I have to speak to."

"To pay me this compliment," Goethe smiled, "you broke all the rules?"

"I'm not in the mood for paying compliments to anybody, not even to you," Graziano said. He glanced out of the window. It was now snowing so hard that he could hardly see the Drottinggatan. "I need an interview with Hamlet's ghost after his return from the undiscovered country."

Graziano's hand was trembling.

"By tomorrow this time," he looked at his watch, "I'll be in that undiscovered country."

"I see." Goethe took note of his own composure with satisfaction. Normally he would have gone to great lengths to avoid contact with a *moribundus.* Even when thinking about such a contingency he used the Latin word for "one who is about to die". The tabloid papers often poked fun at Goethe's attitude to death. He never went to funerals, not even to his mother's, nor to his wife's. Nor did he ever write letters of condolence. Graziano could not be expected to know that.

"What makes you so sure," Goethe asked evenly, "that you're actually facing this...hm...transcendence?"

"Because I was poisoned. I know by whom. And I know why. And please don't tell me I should go to a hospital to have myself pumped out. Geneticists are usually familiar with the human body and I know it's too late. I've had a good run for my money and I'll still be alive for the Prize this afternoon. That's all that matters. I'm not complaining. I've received a number of death threats during the last few weeks and I've been giving the matter some thought. I just want to know *what* and *where* I will be tomorrow afternoon. Of course, this is strictly between you and me. I will count on you not to say a word to anybody while I'm still conscious. Promise."

"I promise," Goethe said. A superstitious man does not fool around in the face of Eternity.

They were passing the Opera House on the *Gustav Adolfs Torg.* He caught a glimpse of a poster announcing *Faust – A Rock Opera.* The Grand Hotel was two minutes away.

"Now answer my question, Goethe."

"I will be pleased to do that," Goethe said with a cheerfulness that stunned him. "At the age of seventy-three one must, of course, think of death occasionally. But this thought never gives me the least uneasiness. I am fully convinced that there is an active Factor X in most of us which is unfathomable and indestructible and which continues its activity in eternity."

"You say 'most of us'."

"I suppose I should have said 'in all of us'. But untalented, boring and lazy people only have microscopic amounts. You may call it by any name you like. Just don't call it the *soul* because you wouldn't want to spend eternity in the company of dreary people who, while still on earth, waste their time thinking about the immortality of their souls. They think about it so much that they can't live their lives properly. The Factor X, even in small amounts, is like the sun, which only seems to set but which, in reality, never sets but shines on for ever and ever. In our galaxy, at least. And I never worry about other suns in other galaxies. I leave that to the specialists. And please, don't ask me for evidence. I have none. All I can say is that it's absolutely impossible for any thinking being to conceive a state of non-being, a cessation of thought and life. The proof is within" − he tapped his chest − "and I'm too proud to look for any conventional evidence."

"That's exactly the kind of talk I hoped to hear from you." Graziano was calming down. Goethe thought, with some satisfaction, that this man had probably not said a kind word to anybody for a long time.

"I cannot conceive of life without activity," he went on. "Life *is* activity. Life is searching, exploring, creating. As you did. You have helped eliminate a universal obstacle to the enjoyment of living − the common cold. Millions will praise you for it. You may rest assured that the superbly run employment bureau in the Beyond will see to it that you'll be able to work there as productively as you did here on earth."

"Thank you, Goethe." Graziano handed a bill to the driver. "You did well."

At the entrance to the packed lobby three teenage girls with autograph books were waiting for the two laureates, ballpoint pens in hand.

Graziano brusquely pushed them aside.

Goethe signed.

Leonora:	*Can you refuse the laurel? Think who gives it.*
Tasso:	*Let me consider what the crown implies.* *How it may change my life.*
Alphonso:	*You will enjoy* *The fame and sure prestige which you now fear.*
Princess *(Holding up the crown):*	*Tasso, will you deny me this rare pleasure* *Of...silently...expressing what I feel?*
Tasso:	*From your hands, then, I will receive the crown* *That I do not deserve. I kneel to you.*
Leonora *(applauding):*	*The first of many crowns to come. Long live* *The poet whose diffidence deserves reward.*

(Goethe, *Torquato Tasso*, Act I, Scene 3, translated by John Prudhoe, Manchester University Press 1979, page 32.)

chapter ten

What's going on here? Am I playing a part written for me by
my friend Eugene Ionesco? Is this the Theatre of the
Absurd? Here I am, a smiling, venerable old Buddha in
fancy dress, ridiculously in love with an enchantingly idealistic and
ambitious girl of tender years whose defining characteristic is a
delightfully protruding upper lip, down there in the audience, in my
direct line of vision, a girl in a lovely light blue dress who gave me a
lovingly moist kiss on the forehead half an hour ago when she greeted
me on the steps of this Concert Hall, a girl who will soon join me to
enable me to complete my *Hauptgeschäft*, the main business of my life.

Well, to start again, here I am, sitting peacefully on this stage next
to an unpleasant man who has fortunately shaved since I saw him last
but who is transmuting silently at the moment of his greatest triumph,
the victim of murder by poison, an event which will please the media
immensely and undoubtedly will be of some interest to Ulrike's
computerized stepfather, the loathsome *Kriminalinspektör* Per
Søderstrom. It is even possible that at the banquet this evening, which
my beloved, my almost-betrothed, will also attend, though only at the
students' table, the murder-victim will still be able to make a speech, as
is required of all living or dying laureates, so that it can be printed in *Les
Prix Nobel*, which the Nobel Foundation puts out every year. But it
seems highly unlikely that the speech, to judge by his performance in
the cab at noon, will be worth printing. If he makes it.

In a few minutes he will have to listen to his introducer, the
chairman of the Nobel Assembly of the Karolinska Institute, explaining

to the world, in incomprehensible Swedish, the significance of his discovery of new possibilities in understanding "the mutation of rhinoviruses by means of identifying a key protein using monoclonal antibodies". And then he will have to step down – "careful, don't fall!" – and exchange polite words with the King, receive his gold medal in a red box and his diploma in a red leather folder, return to his chair on the stage, and continue transfiguring.

And isn't it absurd that I can happily pursue my own thoughts, most of them revolving, directly and indirectly, around *Faust Part Two,* inspired by the life-saving presence of my *inamorata,* and enriched by the metaphysical happenings in my immediate proximity, and can even enjoy, against all expectations, my own coronation? I'm no longer angry at the Swedish Academy which has kept me waiting so long. If I had refused the Prize, the idea of launching Karl on his diplomatic mission would never have occurred to me. No, things are now going surprisingly well. I have nothing but good things to say about my kindly introducer Knut Johannson, the Permanent Secretary of the Swedish Academy, who gave me three glasses of cognac of rare vintage when I visited him in his office after my Nobel Lecture on Monday. The Academy is in the Old Town, two floors above the Stock Exchange, next to the lovely old church, the Storkyke. I admired Johannson's rococo desk, and enjoyed his anecdotes from the two-hundred-year-old Academy. The institution was modeled on the Académie Française, he told me, and is also responsible for keeping the national language pure. I remember everything he told me. The Nobel Committee, he explained, consisted of four of the eighteen members of the Academy, about half of them writers, all Swedish of course, the others scholars in various literary fields, plus one lawyer. It should not be hard to imagine – I recall Knut Johannson smiling ruefully as he told me about this – the torrents of abusive criticism to which they were subjected every year. On one occasion the Swedish press even rebuked them for being a few seconds late when announcing the winner, which they are supposed to do at the stroke of one o'clock every second Thursday in October.

There was no point in arguing with this honourable and civilized man about the lunacy of contemporaries judging contemporaries. The Swedish Academy was not the only lunatic. How can they tell what other people are worth? How can I tell? How valid is my own judgement that I am the greatest? Many people would consider a man like me, a man who prefers the *Blue Danube* to *Lulu,* a sadly fallible judge. They would also think I'm a little strange because, since my two years in Burma, I am addicted to Asian literature, art, movies, restaurants and even music, which bores most of my occidental friends, even today, when large numbers of Asians thrive in every major city in the West.

The point is, none of us should be allowed to judge our contemporaries. Balzac thought that Mrs. Ann Radcliffe's gothic horror stories were better than the novels of his friend Stendhal. Tolstoy, who's been on my mind lately and who believed King Lear was "beneath criticism", was no better in assessing the artists of his own time than the rest of us. The young Albert Einstein was turned down for a job in Switzerland. When Arnold Schoenberg was at the peak of his talent and had serious financial problems, he was turned down for a Guggenheim.

I certainly must not blame the Academy for giving Prizes to what I would consider the wrong people. That's inherent in the process. Moreover, the Academy's taste has to be spiced with politics, since its members are human. Isn't it amazing that sometimes they give Prizes to the right people? I know I'm in good company with Thomas Mann, Boris Pasternak and Winston Churchill. But what about the right people whose names, rumour has it, were submitted but who were turned down? Until this year I was told I fell into that category. I've done a little a research on the subject and I happen to've brought along my list. This is the perfect time to look at it. Here are the names – in alphabetical order:

Anna Akhmatova, W. H. Auden, Thomas Bernhard, Jorge Borges, Bertold Brecht, André Breton, Hermann Broch, Anthony Burgess, Constantine Cavafy, Paul Celan, Anton Chekhov, Paul Claudel, Colette, Joseph Conrad, Sigmund Freud, Robert Frost, Carlo Emilio Gadda, Frederico Garcia Lorca, Maxim Gorki, Günter Grass, Graham Greene, Thomas Hardy, Aldous Huxley, Henrik Ibsen, Henry James, James Joyce, Franz Kafka, Nikolaos Kazantzakis, Arthur Koestler, Milan Kundera, D. H. Lawrence, Doris Lessing, Primo Levi, Norman Mailer, André Malraux, Osip Mandelstam, André Maurois, Alberto Moravia, Robert Musil, Vladimir Nabokov, V. S. Naipaul, Ezra Pound, Marcel Proust, Rainer Maria Rilke, Arthur Schnitzler, Gertrude Stein, Wallace Stevens, August Strindberg, Leo Tolstoy, Mark Twain, Paul Valéry, Tennessee Williams, Virginia Woolf, Emile Zola, Stefan Zweig.

What an incredible performance! No one could conceivably tell...How is it possible? He didn't even fall on the steps to shake hands with the King. His contribution to the forthcoming elimination from the human scene of sore throats, running noses and sneezes dwarfs this achievement!

Listen! The trumpet flourishes for me.

And ah...there it is...that trashy rock-theme for my Gretchen scene which, played by the Stockholm Philharmonic on the balcony up there, sounds like the love-duet from *Tristan and Isolde*.

And remember...Isolde-Gretchen-Ulrike has her eyes on me!

Death of a Fly

With greed she quaffs and quaffs the traitorous drink,
Unceasing, from the start wholly enticed.
She feels so far so good, and every link
In her delicate little legs is paralysed -
No longer deft they are, to groom her wings,
No longer dexterous, to preen her head;
Her life expended, thus, in pleasurings,
Her little feet soon have nowhere to tread;
So does she drink and drink, and while she does,
Comes misty death her myriad eyes to close.

(Goethe, *Selected Poems*, edited by Christopher Middleton, John
Calder, London 1983, page 191. (From Sixteen Parables.))

chapter eleven

T hey were late. Like many of the people who had attended the ceremony, Goethe and Karl, Amalie and Ulrike, wrapped in their heavy coats and guided by Karen Svensen, were supposed to be at the City Hall at six thirty, in twenty minutes. A caravan of buses, Rolls Royces, Mercedes, Cadillacs and Volvos crawled along the freezing, snow-covered Kungsgatan on their way from the Concert Hall to the banquet.

"Wouldn't it be marvellous," Amalie said, "if we could all escape, right now. I happen to know a very expensive restaurant, near a lovely little frozen lake, and we could have a quiet, very alcoholic, very sumptuous smorgasbord."

"Let's go," Goethe agreed enthusiastically.

"It's a nice idea," Ulrike said, "but I'm sure the King and Queen are looking forward to your witty speech, Wolfgang. You mustn't let them down. And after it's all over I'll take you to the Nobel Nightcap. You won't get to bed until four in the morning."

"Where is it?" Amalie asked.

"At the University, in the Engineering Building."

Like the blue carpet in the Concert Hall, the top of the lofty square tower of the brightly lit red-brick City Hall, one of the finest examples of modern architecture in Europe, was decorated by the three gilt crowns of Sweden. On arrival, all the VIPs and their companions were shepherded to the Prince Eugen Gallery on the south side, where pre-banquet cocktails were being served. In the 'twenties Prince Eugen, one of the few artists the royal Bernadotte family had ever produced, painted the murals, scenes from Stockholm's history.

Ulrike went downstairs where the students – altogether about four hundred, a third of all the guests – were gathering. Her table was number forty-seven. It was largely thanks to this impressive contingent of young people, including members of the Students Choral Society, that the atmosphere at the banquet promised to be spirited, notwithstanding the presence of royalty and of most of Sweden's leaders of state, church, the universities, trade unions, the media, plus representatives from the diplomatic corps, and from the police, scrupulously camouflaged in white tie and tails.

The banquet used to be held in the Golden Hall, dominated by a mosaic of the Mälar Queen, symbolizing Stockholm, with the skyscrapers of New York on one side and oriental temples on the other. That is where the ordinary guests, as distinct from VIPs, were now assembling, before proceeding to the accompaniment of organ music, seating diagrams in hand, to the larger Blue Hall, the *Blå Hallen*, blue only because the floor and the Italianesque balconies are blue, the rest is red-brick like most of the City Hall.

In the Prince Eugen Gallery, Goethe, being a mega-VIP, sipping his first glass of champagne, surveyed the scene. Now, where was Edward Graziano? He saw his amiable senior research assistant Robert Lovett, talking to the bird-like Kanya Masao, but not Graziano. What had happened to him on the way between the Concert Hall and the City Hall? In any case, was there really any need for him to be still alive, Goethe wondered, now that he's got his Prize? If he is not, it may well be that the superhuman effort invested in putting on his white tie and tails acted as stimulant for the poison in his system and gave him the *coup de grâce*.

There will be screaming headlines around the world, Goethe mused. What will they say he died of? Poison? At the Karolinska Institute there are certainly enough toxicologists to tell us what kind of poison. But it's not up to the doctors to tell us who did the poisoning, and why. That's up to the computerized *Kriminalinspektör* Per Søderstrom. Who would have thought that my coronation would turn into a detective story? Is it not curious how much I detest my stepfather-in-law-to-be and everything he stands for, without ever having met him? Imagine, to use inhuman computers to solve crimes, the most human of all human activities! But I'd better be careful. Nothing must come between Ulrike and me.

And then there is the immediate question – what about the rest of the week? Will they call off all the remaining events? The banquet tomorrow night, at the Royal Palace? Will I be able to go home early?

Karl gently tapped his shoulder. This time he did not have Amalie in tow – she had been temporarily taken over by Ramsey Mansbridge – but rather a stunning beauty, magnificently bejewelled. "Wolfgang," Karl said, "*Madame* says she is too well brought up to speak to you directly. Her name is Yvonne de Beauchamps. Be careful. Her husband is the French Ambassador. We don't need any diplomatic complications."

Goethe bowed to her. Karl excused himself.

"*Enchanté, madame,*" he said.

"I want to tell you," she said, "that you look even better *in persona* than on the screen."

He relished her velvety voice and deliciously nerve-tingling perfume.

"You are very kind, *madame*. It must be your beauty which is reflected in my face."

"No one else but you, my dear Goethe, could have thought of such a graceful compliment, however untrue. No wonder I've been admiring you since I was fifteen when I first read your *Werther*. I decided then and there that one day I simply had to meet the man who wrote that lovely book, never mind how much the effort of finding you would cost me. I'm going to snatch you away from your famous friend Karl. "

"*Madame,*" Goethe said solemnly, "I'm very expensive."

"I know that," she retorted, "but I can afford you."

"I will have to request the President of the Banque de France to confirm that statement in writing. I need to know things black on white. In the meantime, may I get you another glass of champagne?"

He tried to catch the attention of a waiter, but he was not the only one. His rival was Donald Heath, who was having a lively argument with the Archbishop of Uppsala. After a waiter had served both of them, Heath turned to Goethe and Yvonne de Beauchamps.

"Please help me," he said. "I'm afraid I don't know how to handle the Archbishop. His Grace is trying to give me a sermon on matters I know far better than he."

"I was simply saying," the white-haired, pink-faced cleric stretched out his hands, "that the penalty rules in Swedish hockey were different from the Canadian rules. But the distinguished Professor Sonoluminescence begs to differ."

"His Grace is being stubborn about this," Heath shook his head in comic desperation, "because last week we beat the Swedish team in Winnipeg. Your Grace, you're a terrible loser!"

Before Goethe had a chance to display to Yvonne de Beauchamps his well-honed talents as a practising diplomat, Amalie arrived to announce that the procession was about to start.

The entrance to the Blue Hall was heavily ritualized, once again according to the precedence set by the terms of Alfred Nobel's will — Physics, Chemistry, Medicine, Literature — and, as a post-Nobel afterthought, Economics. The will did not specify that, in the procession to the banquet, the Queen was to walk in first, and King last, the Queen with the winner of the Physics Prize, the King with the winner of the Chemistry Prize, whatever the respective gender. But that practice was established by tradition. Nor was there any protocol about who would walk in with the literary winner. Goethe quickly managed to persuade one of the banquet organizers to allow the gorgeous Yvonne de Beauchamps to remain at his side. However, it was made clear she would not be his dinner companion. Queen Silvia was.

This year the organizers had encountered serious protocol problems in other respects. Donald Heath had no legitimate spouse. His illegitimate spouse Catherine, who had tactfully stayed at home, happened to be the legitimate spouse of the American medical laureate, Edward Graziano, who was conspicuously absent. Regiments of Nobel officials were at this very moment checking with the hotel and wondering whether to break into his room.

The scene in the Blue Hall was splendid, crowded, confused and, especially in the students' areas, noisy. The lights were bright enough to take care of the requirements of television. Cables were carefully hidden so that the guests and waiters would not stumble over them. The tables, altogether sixty-one of them, were covered with flowers, "graciously offered", as the menu noted, by an Italian travel bureau. The decorations and dinnerware were exquisite. In the centre was the long table for eighty VIPs, including the King and Queen, to be seated opposite one another in the middle. Experts had systematically drilled two hundred uniformed waiters, volunteers from all over Sweden, for days in advance. Later they were to receive excellent reviews for their balletic skills and for their admirable ability to remain cool even, as we shall see, under heavy strain.

Menu

Suprême de turbot froid aux oeufs d'Arlette
Sauce hollandaise
Selle de veau rôti
Sauce aux morilles
Pommes sautées
Salade de haricots verts
Parfait glace Nobel
Petits fours

Vins

H. G. Mumm, Cordon Rouge, Brut
Château Trinité-Valrose 1990
Eau Minerale de Ramiösa

Café

Baron Ôtard, Fine Champagne, V.S.O.P.
Liqueur Mandarine Napoléon

Buffet

Bols Silver Top Dry Gin
Long John Whisky

Karl had not mentioned even to Goethe that he recently discovered he was distantly related to the handsome and sports-loving King Carl XVI Gustav. The King's mother happened to be Princess Sibylla of Saxe-Coburg-Gotha. Karl had never met the King, nor did he on this occasion. Most probably the King would have been far more interested in Goethe, with whom he shared an interest in nature conservation and the environment, rather than Karl, even if he was a rich relative.

Queen Silvia, a German commoner of uncommon beauty who had been in public relations before her marriage, had met the King during the Munich Olympics in 1972. It was a fairy-tale romance which delighted the whole world. They were married in 1976. Her name had been Silvia Renate Sommerlath. No professional training could have qualified her better than public relations for the duties she was to perform during a succession of Intellectual Olympics, especially this year, when the jewel in her native country's literary crown and the most glamourous television star was to be her dinner companion. After all, she even had to study him at school.

However, having the right to sit next to him was by no means a matter of royal prerogative. On the contrary. Protocol demanded the Queen sit with the chemistry laureate, Elizabeth Priestley. When she asked to be permitted to break with this tradition and sit next to Goethe, on the grounds of his unique celebrity and their common origins, the officials said no, sorry, impossible, that could not conceivably be done. Only by appealing directly to Baron Lennert, whose daughter had been in the Swedish Olympic swimming team in Munich and had played a pivotal role in the royal romance, did she manage to have her wish granted.

In the end this was the solution: The King sat between Elizabeth Priestley and Kanya Okita, Donald Heath at Priestley's left. Opposite them, from left to right, were Yvonne de Beauchamps, Goethe, Queen Silvia and Edward Graziano, if he turned up. Masao Okita was placed at the left end of the table between the daughter of the *Talman*, the President of the Swedish parliament, and the imposing Maria Gösting, the wife of the President of the Bank of Sweden.

The meal began. The wine was poured. Everybody sang *The King's Song*. At first, the conversation was distinctly more polite and formal at the VIPs' table than among the students, from whom waves of raucous laughter began to emanate as soon as everybody sat down.

At long last, after about five minutes – Goethe caught his breath and narrowed his eyes in disbelief – three Nobel officials escorted Edward Graziano to his seat, very close to him, right at the other side of Queen Silvia. *"Mon dieu,"* Goethe whispered, totally fascinated. Graziano was unsteady on his feet – the officials had to support him by his elbows. One of them went to the King and whispered a few words to him, and then to the Queen.

Graziano, properly attired but looking ghastly, took his assigned place. He did not excuse himself. He did not greet Her Majesty. He simply sat down. Goethe was at her other side. He could not see Graziano, like a sleepwalker, taking his napkin, unfolding it, putting it on his lap and staring in front of him. But the Queen could see it and was seriously concerned, particularly when she couldn't help noticing that his hands were shaking violently.

"Let me tell you what happened to me last Friday on the SAS plane from London." Elizabeth Priestley addressed the whole table while, to her delight, the television cameras zoomed in on her. She may have arranged this beforehand with the producer. "It's true, isn't it" – she turned to the King – "that you, Your Majesty, were on the plane with my husband and me?"

"Yes, indeed."

"In the plane, the stewardess made an announcement. She said – you were there, Your Majesty, you heard it – 'Ladies and Gentlemen. Would you please pay attention. I have an important announcement to make. We have on board on this flight a very distinguished passenger.' Somebody had pointed you out to me when we were looking for our seats – first class, thanks to the Nobel Foundation, for both of us – so naturally I expected her to say. 'We are deeply honoured to have on board on this flight His Majesty King Carl Gustav of Sweden.' But that's not what she said. She said, 'We are deeply honoured to have on board this year's winner of the Nobel Prize for Chemistry, Elizabeth Priestley and her distinguished husband, Professor Ramsey Mansbridge. Not a word about you, Your Majesty. Isn't that true, Your Majesty?"

During this lively discourse – which was greeted with appropriate laughter and applause, including His and Her Majesties' Edward Graziano noiselessly slid under the table. At first nobody at the table noticed it, so captivated were they by Elizabeth Priestley. The television producer in the booth, however, saw it and quickly ordered his cameramen to move away from Elizabeth Priestley, in the direction of the swooning Californian. This camera-move attracted Goethe's attention. He leaned back in his seat, to look behind the Queen's back, at the very moment when the Queen herself became aware of her dinner companion's sudden absence. Practical as ever, she quickly grasped the situation, or at least whatever was graspable at that moment, and collected a dozen napkins to put under his head. Yvonne de Beauchamps also became aware of the commotion and rose, quickly followed by the King who hurriedly summoned a waiter. Donald Heath jumped up and ran around the long table. He loosened Graziano's collar, undid his white tie and opened his waistcoat. All this on live television.

So the poor man had suffered a fainting spell. Obviously he was not well – which was evidently the reason why he was late. No doubt within a few minutes he would be carried out on a stretcher to some sort of first-aid station. In a hard-drinking country like Sweden, at every banquet presumably there are at least a dozen persons who drink too much and must be carried out.

Goethe rose and slowly removed himself from the Grim Reaper's stage effects.

It is better you suffer an injustice rather than the world suffers lawlessness. Therefore, obey the law.

(Maxim 832. Goethes Werke, Kleine Ausgabe, *Maxime und Reflektionen,* Bibliographisches Institut, Leipzig.)

––––––––––

If I don't like a thing I leave it alone or do it better.

(Maxim 934. Goethes Werke, Kleine Ausgabe, *Maxime und Reflektionen,* Bibliographisches Institut, Leipzig.)

chapter twelve

Where was Ulrike? Goethe felt a manic urge to tell Ulrike what was happening.

Where was table forty-seven?

Goethe asked one of the waiters.

Ah, there she was, in light blue. She looked absolutely lovely. At the ceremony her brown hair had still been in place, well kempt. Now it was tousled, the way it usually was – just marvellous. She was the only girl at the table in formal dress. All the others wore short dresses, and the boys ties and ordinary suits or jackets. Everybody was drinking beer. (Goethe had an aversion to beer.) They were, very obviously, having considerably more fun than the VIPs. Ulrike was engaged in an animated conversation with a pale, blond boy with freckles, a little too engaged for Goethe's liking. His throat was dry with excitement.

Some students jumped up, delighted that the wandering icon would single out their table.

Others remained seated. "Look who's here," one of them said.

Only then did Ulrike look up. Tactful as always, Goethe gave her an impersonal smile. She opened her mouth slightly. Both concealed that they knew each other.

"We are honoured," a tall, gaunt-faced student declared, apparently meaning it. No TV monitor was in sight. They had seen nothing of Graziano's collapse. "Everyone knows you're man of good taste, *maestro*. You prefer us to all the people at your table. I don't blame you. Come and sit down with us. The television people will love this."

"Thank you."

Goethe gave Ulrike a moment to greet him – which she did not –
before he squeezed in between two students who made room for him.

"I've always wanted to ask you," a dark-haired beauty, with a slight
accent, perhaps Middle Eastern, asked, "whether you know all your
poems by heart."

"I'm afraid not."

"Do you enjoy reading them?"

"Some of them. I like reading them aloud, to my friends. And do
you know something? I only reread my first novel once. Some years
ago."

"What novel was that?"

"Werther. I hate to tell you that I was so moved that I couldn't finish
it. I lived through all the agony I suffered when I wrote it. That was very
long ago."

There was a moment's respectful silence while Ulrike realised that
he was leaving it to her to make the first move. She cleared her throat
and announced to the table, in a clear voice, "I think Goethe came over
because he needed a change of scene. And I'm probably the only
young person in this room he knows. You see, he's a friend of my
family's."

"Really?" the boy with the freckles asked.

"Yes, that's perfectly true," Goethe said. He decided he had been
considerate long enough. "Ulrike, may I drag you away from your
friends? I promise to bring you back in a few minutes."

"Of course."

Perhaps, Ulrike thought, her mother had told Goethe she had
agreed to switching universities for a semester or two and spending
some time near him. But was this the moment to talk about it?

"I hope I didn't embarrass you," Goethe said making his way
between the tables while she followed him.

"Certainly not. Please don't worry."

"Do you mind if we go to the VIP lounge up there?"

He pointed to the Prince Eugen Gallery.

"Good idea."

They went up the stairs. A few people sat at the bar, having escaped
for a few moment's relief from boring dinner companions they had not
chosen. Goethe and Ulrike took their seats above the balcony, the Blue
Hall below them. He ordered two glasses of Aquavit and told her about
the imminent death of Edward Graziano – perhaps he had already
died. First, she wanted to interrupt and say, "Please – why are you

telling me all this?" But then she got caught up in the story.

"Wolfgang, you have to go to the police. You have to tell them what the man told you in the cab."

Goethe realised what she meant was going to her stepfather Per Søderstrom, the loathsome *Kriminalinspektör*.

"My dear" – he stopped himself from saying "my dear child" – "I have absolutely no intention of doing any such thing. I have more important things to do."

When Goethe noticed that Ulrike was genuinely, profoundly shocked, he knew he had made a mistake – but it was too late. Once said, it could not be unsaid. He had simply made an error – making errors was, after all, only the reverse side of constantly striving. He now had to correct the error. That was difficult but not impossible. The truth was that he had nothing against the police as such. He had an *idée fixe* about Søderstrom.

"I can't believe that you would say such a thing, Wolfgang. You, of all people, who tells everybody to work hard and do their job. What could be more important?"

How could he answer that? *Faust Part Two*? No, the only way to save the situation was to make light of it and lie a little.

"My antipathy to the police happens to be one of my very few weaknesses. No doubt this has to do with things that I saw when I was young, living in a police state before my family and I got out, before it evolved into a criminal state. It's just stuck with me."

"I think that's a terrible excuse. From a man like you! That was – let me see – fifty, sixty years ago. No one knows better than you that the world has changed. No, I think you just don't want to bother."

"You may be right, my dear. Have another drink."

"No thanks." An idea suddenly occurred to her. "You know that the head of anti-terrorist operations of the Security Service of the Swedish Police is my stepfather?"

"Yes. Your mother told me."

"And that he's Sweden leading authority on crime detection?"

"Yes, my dear. I know."

"And this may very well come under him?"

"I suppose so."

"Would you mind if tomorrow morning I go to him and tell him what you told me?"

"Only if by then Graziano is dead."

"Naturally. Would you mind?"

"Why should I mind? Do what your conscience tells you to do."

"Thank you."

If she goes ahead and hands this to Søderstrom, Goethe thought, I will have to hurry up and find out who poisoned Graziano, and why, myself, in my own way, whatever that is — before Søderstrom's computers give him the answer. Only that way can I correct my error and recover my position *vis-à-vis* Ulrike. It will be a highly symbolic, historic race between the human way and the non-human way, an allegory worthy of the man who will soon complete *Faust Part Two*. The human way had better win.

Both cheered up considerably. Ulrike took his hand on the way down the stairs. Once they were in the hall, making their way towards table forty-seven, she let go. "Don't forget," she said as she sat down again next to the freckled boy, "you've still got to make a witty speech. Do you know what you're going to say?"

"I'll think of something," he replied as he took his leave, "if there's enough champagne left."

"If I'd been born in England, I would have been born a rich duke, or rather a bishop with an annual income of £30,000."
"That's very nice," I said. "But suppose you had not won the lottery? There are always infinitely more losers than winners."
"My dear friend," Goethe replied, "I fully realise that. But do you think I would have been so foolish as to have been born a loser?"

(J. P. Eckermann, *Conversations with Goethe,* F. A. Brockhaus Wiesbaden 1959, page 558.)

chapter thirteen

Reprint from *Les Prix Nobel 1992*
Johann Wolfgang von Goethe

Your Majesties, Your Royal Highnesses, Ladies and Gentlemen.

I think I can speak for all the laureates, present and absent, who were honoured today when I say that we are deeply grateful for having been chosen to benefit from he great legacy left to the world by Alfred Nobel. We also give thanks for having been supplied with the requisite amounts of DNA which made it possible for us to be considered for the Prize, and to the unfathomable and indestructible Something in the human spirit that has whipped the DNA into shape.

But that is not all we needed to make it possible for us to be here tonight. We also had to have access to *money*. I have no doubt that every one of us has, like myself, at least one rich friend. I think I am probably a typical case. I have a very rich friend. Every clever word I've ever written or said has cost him a fortune. My former colleague Bertold Brecht – I never met him, he was not really my type – once observed that a thorough study of Marxism costs at least forty thousand gold marks. From my own experience I can add that my study of life has cost my friend infinitely more.

Then there is another thing we needed. We needed the right moment to be born. George Washington's inheritance was King George III of England. Napoleon's was the French Revolution.

Nietzsche's inheritance was Schopenhauer's misanthropy. Kafka's was Nietzsche's saying "Yes". My inheritance – I now speak primarily but not entirely as a scientist – was the all-pervasive triumph of computer technology which has taken the humanity – the surprise, the joy, the humour – out of most research. The new world of computers seems to have forgotten who's the sorcerer and who's the apprentice. I was confronted with an ocean of joyless data in my work in environmental geochemistry. The data overwhelmed me and made it impossible for me to reach my goal, which was to discover that the microbes who dwell deep in the planetary crust and are creating much of the Earth's surface actually make love in order to multiply. I have not been able to document this, even though, as the world knows, I look for love everywhere. I must now leave this task to my successors. They will have to prove that the world is based on love. After all, scientists invariably find what they are looking for, if they have enough rich friends. They know perfectly well that first comes the intuition, then the observation, then the scientific proof. As my Mephisto says, all theory is grey, the tree of life is golden-green. First comes the rich life experience with its green and golden colours. Then comes, limping along many miles behind, the drab, grey theory, proving the green, golden observations "correct" – and thereby qualifying for the Nobel Prize.

The question remains how the grey and golden life experiences enter the human brain, and stay there. In 1932, the Nobel Committee at the Karolinska Institute awarded the Prize jointly to the English neurologists Sir Charles Scott Sherrington and Lord Adrian, for their "discovery regarding the function of neurons", and in 1963 it recognized the equally important contributions made by the Australian neurologist Sir John Carew Eccles. It was in relation to those three that a philosopher once asked me, somewhat frivolously, "Why do all neurologists go mystical?" That was a reference to their dualism between brain and mind which in Eccles's view was "transduced" in the synapse. I doubt whether Sherrington, Adrian and Eccles would have answered that philosopher friend of mine, "All right, call us mystics, if you like." No, they would have said, "There are limits to what we scientists know at this time. It just so happens the brain is a very mysterious, very tricky organ. There's no need to call us names."

I'm in a much more fortunate position than these three eminent neurologists. I am Goethe. I am allowed certain liberties. I am allowed to be mysterious, even mystical, and, no doubt, if I'm ever able to write

Faust Part Two, I shall be called a mystificator. When the American geneticist Barbara McClintock, who received her Nobel Prize in 1983, spoke of the need to have a "feeling for the organism – that is the first and crucial necessity for a biologist", she was, in a sense, a mystic, though no doubt she would have rejected the label, vehemently.

I once had a long talk with Salvador Dali. I told him how much I admired his painstaking technique – he did not usually work with quick, stunning strokes, like Picasso. He spent long hours filling in the details. "For me," Dali said, "it's either easy or it's impossible."

I see you are becoming impatient. I don't blame you. You want your dessert. And you think I'm rambling on only in order to gain time because I don't know how to end. But you're wrong. I do. I want to end by speaking in praise of error. None of us would ever have qualified for a Nobel Prize if we hadn't spent our lives committing error after error. Every human being, even those who have not – or not yet – won a Nobel, has a *self,* a product of experience, continually growing, continually correcting errors.

Thank you, Your Majesties, Your Royal Highnesses, Ladies and Gentlemen. I had been afraid that, after the many stirring events of the day, I would find making this speech impossible. But, thanks to your gracious hospitality, patience and kindness, I have found it easy.

Bon appétit!

While acknowledging the applause, Goethe glanced across the room to table forty-seven. His fragile heart missed a beat when he noticed that Ulrike was finding something the blond boy with freckles said hilarious. Was it at his expense? If she brings that boy along to the Nobel Nightcap, to which she had promised to take him, Amalie and Karl after the banquet, how would he survive?

The three other laureates still in the Hall followed Goethe. Donald Heath told a few anecdotes about his attempts to explain to the German chancellor Helmut Kohl what sonoluminescence was. Elizabeth Priestley described in meticulous detail the many beds, and the circumstances in which she slept in them, and at what moments, she dreamed of receiving the Nobel Prize, and Masao Okita gave a lively account of the reversal of roles during the 1980s when the U.S., formerly the world's greatest net creditor nation, became the world's greatest net debtor nation, with Japan going through the opposite motions. He was among the few who found his talk witty.

As the dinner proceeded, the decibels rose in synch with the intake of food and alcohol, even at Goethe's table.

"I understand, Herr von Goethe," Queen Silvia said, "you will soon give us a conclusion to your *Faust*." She had to raise her voice because the Students Choral Society had just begun singing.

"I hope so, Your Majesty," Goethe said. "That depends very much on conditions over which I have only limited control."

"We are all looking forward to it so much. So I am sure are the millions of children all over the world who so much enjoyed the First Part."

"I will do my best," Goethe assured her.

Yvonne de Beauchamps had followed the conversation closely, even though the Queen sat Goethe's other side. Since he had returned to the table after his little chat with Ulrike, he found her perfume more deliciously nerve-tingling than ever.

"What about Gretchen?" she asked. "I'm sure you've heard that a number of women's organizations in the United States are demanding that you undo the damage you did to their cause in the First Part."

"No, I hadn't heard that." Goethe frowned. "I'll certainly try and oblige them. Perhaps, in my final scene, I'll have Gretchen forgive Faust and welcome him into Heaven."

"I'm sure they'll love that," Yvonne de Beauchamps declared. "That'll be very good for the box office. All you need now is a final line about the Eternal Feminine, or something."

A blaring trumpet fanfare prevented Goethe from replying.

The lights dimmed. At the command of an all-powerful sergeant-major in cook's uniform, two hundred waiters took positions along the banquet tables. Each held a silver tray high up in the air. On it were mountains of Parfait glace Nobel, each crowned with an "N".

At the command of another blare of fanfares, they began their assault on the guests.

After the banquet was over, Goethe had to submit to three interviews and after that to the obligatory photo-taking with the King and Queen.

He managed to snatch Karl away from Amalie for a moment and sat down with him alone in a corner. He told him about Graziano – and about his talk with Ulrike who no doubt would take up the matter with her stepfather tomorrow. If Graziano dies.

"Well, they'll try and stop the police, of course, if they can."

"Who will stop them?"

"Whatever minister is in charge, Wolfgang." Karl was in his element. "Maybe the Prime Minister. You've got to realise that the Swedes will engineer a colossal cover-up. Can you imagine what this means to them? A Nobel laureate taken out, poisoned, murdered, assassinated, terminated, erased, eliminated, massacred on the very day of his anointment? What it means to the whole Nobel industry? Their most important export! They're no fools. They know that henceforth any laureate will think twice before coming here for a Nobel. They will say, 'Thank you very much, please fax the award!' Why should they expose themselves to poison?"

"Good thinking, Karl. I never thought of that. All I thought of was that I've got find the murderer before Søderstrom does."

"Of course. I know you. You want to impress the girl."

"My friend," Goethe was amused, "you think you know me. But you got it all wrong. You don't understand it's a race between the man who wrote *Faust Part One* and the author of *Computational Logic and Crime Detection*. The whole world is at stake."

"Is that all?" Karl laughed. "Well then, we'd better be prepared. I'm going to conduct my own investigation. I'll have to move with lightning speed. The first thing I'll do is establish the motive. I will immediately mobilize my bureau in San Francisco. It covers Stanford University in Palo Alto. I will ask them to wire me everything they can find out about Graziano. Suspect number one of course will be Donald Heath who, as we've been told repeatedly, has stolen Graziano's wife, Catherine. For all you know, Elizabeth Priestley and Masao Okita also have motives."

"Not so fast, please."

"I know, you've always had your rich friend do your fast thinking for you. I will ask my London and Tokyo people to find out all they can about Elizabeth Priestley and Masao Okita. I will ask them to give this matter top priority and let me have the results by Sunday morning, Swedish time. That's the 13th. By the way, as you will see, December 13th – Saint Lucia Day – is a very big day in Sweden. We should have no trouble getting the stuff by then. That gives them plenty of time. They're used to that sort of thing from me. They say they love me for it. For all I know, they're telling the truth. Once we have the motive, we find the proof. That's the easy part. First the basic fact-finding and the green and golden delving below the surface to find out what the basic facts mean, then the drab, grey proof. We'll publish it around the world. The Swedes won't know what hit them."

———

At about one o'clock they were driven to the Engineering Building at the University for the Nobel Nightcap. A big lecture hall had been converted into a disco. The boy with freckles came along, but throughout the proceedings both he and Ulrike treated Goethe with consideration and respect.

They were placed in the hands of students in T-shirts and jeans. As a courtesy to their English-speaking guests some of them wore around their necks fake gold medals in English saying "Seventh Gold Star for Prehistoric Trigonometry" and "Consolation Prize for Babylonian Hermeneutics".

It was not only the students who had been at the banquet who had managed to change their clothes. Masao Okita, too, and his wife, Kanya, had quickly gone to the hotel, leaving the taxi waiting at the door, and slipped on loud Hawaiian shirts. Donald Heath put on a green, long-sleeved baseball shirt with "Blue Jays" prominently inscribed in the front and the back and a baseball cap. Elizabeth Priestley wore a dark grey gown which looked like a hand-me-down from her cleaning lady. Amalie, too, managed to change somewhere into a blouse and slacks. Only Goethe and Karl were still in tails. Goethe decided there was only one way to make the entertainment tolerable that was to join in the fun and games.

The stage was a boxing ring, with an upright piano in a corner. First, students performed unintelligible skits in Swedish. Then they were determined to demonstrate that the world's greatest intellects were incapable of cutting apart and nailing together again a simple piece of wood at an acceptable speed. To try and disprove this ludicrous thesis, the laureates had to form two teams. Since Edward Graziano was unavailable and his handsome assistant Robert Lovett could not be persuaded to pinch-hit for him it was decided, after protracted and noisy negotiations, that Physics and Chemistry would compete against Literature and Economics.

The two natural sciences might conceivably have won if they had not had so much to drink and had not wasted so much valuable time arguing about Donald Heath's baseball cap which he refused to take off. Priestley stubbornly insisted the cap would bring their team bad luck. Goethe, oblivious to constituting fifty percent of the opposing team, declared that Elizabeth was right. He was in favour of superstition *en principe,* he said. If Elizabeth thought the baseball cap would bring their team bad luck her view had to be taken seriously. It was human nature to be superstitious, he explained, because if you tried to chase superstition out through the front door it would sooner or later return through the back door. Then he reversed himself and pronounced a brand-new Goethe-discovery – Superstition brings bad luck. At last the MC blew the whistle and said it was time for the Sofie Hess Song.

Protesting vociferously – Donald Heath actually had to be forcibly removed by two muscular engineering students – the laureates descended from the stage and took their seats in the front row. Ulrike sat down with the blond boy with freckles. Someone made the mistake of handing Goethe an overflowing mug of beer, which spilled over on his pants. Of course he would not touch the beer. They tried to make good by bringing him a bottle of cognac.

The MC – a tall, bony medical student who spoke excellent English – stepped on the stage. He had his arm around a sad girl with dark hair who looked like Edith Piaf and carried a bouquet of withered roses. The girl never smiled. Her name, he said, was Ingrid Bergsen.

"Ladies and gentleman," the MC began. "This young orphan is about to give the first performance of the Sofie Hess Song. It will soon be number one on the top-tens all over the world. The song was specially composed for this historic occasion. You are enormously privileged to be present at this moment. Unfortunately the song's in Swedish, so you will forgive me for first giving you the background in English.

"You may not know that Alfred Nobel was an unhappy, miserable genius who never married. He died in 1896, but until 1950 nobody had ever heard of Sofie Hess, nor of any other woman in his life, other than his mother. He had no time for women. He worked fifteen hours a day. He was some sort of socialist, and pacifist, but he believed in elected dictators and thought only those people should have a vote who belonged to an educated minority. He was always traveling around and lived in hotel rooms. He hated hotel rooms. He spoke five languages. Victor Hugo called him 'Europe's richest vagabond'. His company was the first modern multinational corporation. He hated business. He was such a prodigious inventor that he scored one invention for every month of his working life. He held three hundred and fifty-five patents. He invented synthetic leather. He invented synthetic rubber. He invented rockets for rocketry. He invented dynamite for peaceful purposes. Not for the military. Not for the terrorists who in 1881 used it to blow up Czar Alexander II, for starters.

"He met Sofie Hess in 1876 at the resort of Baden near Vienna, when he was forty-three. Not Baden-Baden – Baden. She was a flower girl of twenty. I mean, she sold flowers. The intellectual gulf between them was insurmountable.

"In 1950, our Nobel Foundation, right here in Stockholm," the MC continued, "revealed the existence of two hundred and eighteen letters written by Alfred Nobel to Sofie Hess, over a period of seventeen years. In her letters to him she mostly asked for money, though he had set her up very generously. Let me read to you a section from one of his last letters to her, which will explain why he did not leave his money to her, but instead dreamed up his greatest invention – the Nobel Prize.

"You will never be able to understand me on a deeper level. You understand only what suits you. You are not capable of grasping that for many years I have sacrificed my time, my reputation, all my associations with the educated world and finally my business – all for a self-indulgent child who is not even capable of discerning the selflessness of these acts...I am ending, my dear, good, tender Sofie, with the heartfelt hope that your life will be better than mine, and that you will never be struck by the feeling of debasement that embitters my days.'[1] "

The accompanist struck a few melancholy chords.

"Ingrid will now sing the Sofie Hess Song. She'll tell the world what Alfred Nobel was like in bed."

Before she could start Baron Gunnar Lennert, his face ashen, climbed up to the stage.

"It has just been announced," he said, "that Edward Graziano has died at the Karolinska Hospital. The cause of death was heart failure."

[1]   Kenne Fant, *Alfred Nobel; A Biography,* translated by Marianna Ruuth, Arcade Publishing, New York 1993, page 146.

A pleasant landscape. Faust couched on flowery grass, tired, restless, trying to sleep.
Dawn
Chorus of Spirits:

The hours are spent. Pain and joy have vanished. You will be strong and well again. Let yourself feel it coming. Trust the new daylight. See, the valleys are turning green, the little hills are swelling, showing their trees and shade, and in waves of swaying silver the season's crop advances.

To get your wish, your every wish, turn your eyes to the light. Your bonds are fragile. Sleep is a husk, throw it off. Lose no time, be bold, let others doubt and linger. A real man can achieve anything if he takes hold intelligently and doesn't delay.

(*Faust Part Two,* Scene 26, translated by Barker Fairley, University of Toronto Press 1970, page 82.)

chapter fourteen

Goethe's dream:

It is spring. He is lying in an Alpine meadow, surrounded by yellow and blue flowers, exhausted and restless, trying to sleep. He hears snatches of a soothing movement from a Mahler symphony. The flowers exude a lovely smell – health-giving, invigorating. He tries to remember how he got to the Alps, why he is there when he is supposed to be in Singapore. Maybe he is in the Himalayas? How did Mahler get to the Himalayas? The Lord Buddha suddenly appears out of nowhere, wearing his usual benign smile. "I am the God of Healing and Forgetting," he says in Frankfurt dialect. "You need me."

Goethe woke up, stretched, rubbed his eyes and looked at his watch. It was just before nine o'clock. He'd had only four hours' sleep. Good, he didn't have a headache. Quite an achievement. Buddha was right, forgetting is healing. He was going to begin *Faust Part Two* with a waking-up monologue, in an idyllic landscape, his guilt feelings towards Gretchen erased. If Ulrike changes her mind – he was beginning to have premonitions of disaster – would he ever be able to forget her?

Oh, what a heart-breaking story that was, the story of

Sofie Hess. He remembered a line from his novel *Wilhelm Meister*. "What business of yours is it if I love you?" Did that apply to him and Ulrike? How cruel of those students to make fun of Sofie Hess and Nobel. Young people have no heart, he thought. That's why he always said old people were better equipped than young people to do the important things in this world. The Chinese were right about that.

The telephone rang. It was his son, August, who – together with his wife, Ottlie – was looking after his affairs in Oberreifenberg. Their marriage was notoriously bad, but both had little trouble finding diversions outside. Last summer, when Goethe went for an evening stroll in the garden after the sun had gone down, he nearly stumbled over August making love to a not very pretty actress. With two fingers he delicately picked up her panties, which she had thrown on the grass, and said "Please carry on, my children. Don't let me distract you," and continued on his stroll, much amused.

"Papa," August was thirty-four, "I just wanted to know how you feel this morning. I watched the news last night and noticed you got up even before the poor man was carried out. Did you know how serious it was?"

"Yes, my son. I did."

"So why did you get up so quickly?"

Goethe took a deep breath. August knew Ulrike. The one thing he and Ottilie dreaded most in life was his father getting married again and doing them out of their inheritance. Goethe knew that.

"I wanted to speak to your future stepmother."

"To whom did you say?" August asked.

"I wanted to speak to Ulrike."

There was a short pause.

"Why don't you just sleep with the little girl and get it over with?"

August must have had a few drinks already. He would never had had the courage to say this to his father while sober.

"Why do you begrudge your old father a few years of marital bliss?" he asked

"Bliss, yes," August shouted. "Have all the bliss you like. With little girls and big girls. But why marital? Why is marital suddenly so important? I was seventeen before you married my mother. It was a matter of complete indifference to you how she felt about being a single mother."

"My dear boy, before your mother met me she worked in a factory. I married her in the face of heavy, heavy opposition from Karl and from every snob in the whole, wide world. She never uttered a word of reproach to me. All she asked for was my love. And that she got."

"Not only she."

Goethe let that pass.

"Mother never complained," August continued. "But I know she suffered. And so did I. My teachers made my life miserable in school, just because my parents weren't married. You thought they'd fall all over themselves. After all, I was the son of the great Goethe, the author of *Faust*. Well, they didn't. You thought – if you gave the matter any thought at all – this was the twentieth century and people didn't care any more about that sort of thing. But they do. You've never understood what goes on under your very nose. For seventeen years you thought marriage was an empty formality. Meaningless. And now suddenly...My dear Papa, I think you give egoism a bad name."

"On the contrary," Goethe replied gravely, "thanks to me, the causal connection between egoism and extraordinary achievement has become universally recognized. Do you have any messages for me?"

"Yes, there's a fax from Torelli in Rome. They are restoring the southern wall of the Coliseum and want you to join their team of experts."

"When does he want me to fly down?"

"Thursday week."

"Tell him yes, I'll come."

"When are you returning home?"

"It's hard to say. Maybe on Monday."

"Well, I hope you'll enjoy the rest of your time."

Goethe put the received down and turned on the radio to listen to the BBC nine o'clock news.

Stockholm – Medical laureate Edward Graziano's sudden death of heart failure at Nobel Prize banquet in Stockholm. Short commentary to follow after the news. Full tribute at noon.

London – New hope of peace in Ulster.

Moscow – Yeltsin fights back, fears violence on the streets.

Brussels – Prime Minister John Major clashes with Jacques Delors, President of the European Commission

Copenhagen – Denmark looms large in search of Maastricht Solution

Hong Kong – Talks on transition stall

St. Petersburg – DNA tests identify Tsarina's bones

Now – a short commentary on the death of the geneticist Edward Graziano in Stockholm.

No laureate has ever died during the Nobel Week, he heard, even though the age of many was far more advanced than Edward Graziano's. The American medical laureate Peyton Rous was eighty-seven in 1966 when he got his Nobel Prize for his discovery of tumour-inducing viruses. He lived for another four years. The Italian chemistry laureate Giulio Natta received the Chemistry Prize in 1963 for his discovery of high polymers. Admittedly he was only sixty, but he suffered so badly from Parkinson's disease that he managed to reach his chair on the stage of the Concert Hall only with the greatest effort, aided by his son. When he was asked to step down he nearly fell. King Gustaf Vl Adolf, who was eighty-one, ran up the stairs with his long legs, two steps at a time, to hand him the medal. The audience burst into prolonged applause – for the King as much as for the suffering chemist who lived for another sixteen years.

Goethe turned the dial. He caught a news program from Hamburg.

At this moment Baron Gunnar Lennert and his steering committee are meeting with the American Ambassador and representatives of the royal family to confirm the commemorative arrangements that have been planned. They envisage that tomorrow, Saturday, at ten in the morning, there will be a non-denominational memorial service at the U.S. Embassy. The traditional banquet planned for tonight, Friday, at the Royal Palace, will take place. The Ambassador takes the view that it would not have been in the spirit of Edward Graziano's life and work to call it off, and the delegates from the Palace willingly agree to hold it as scheduled. Normally there would be no speeches, but this time Sten Holmgren, the Chairman of the Nobel Assembly of the Karolinska Institute and professor of Clinical Physiology, will deliver the eulogy. The events scheduled between now and next Monday when the laureates are expected to leave, will take place as planned, including the taping on Saturday of the Round Table discussion "Science and Man." It is hoped that Robert Lovett can be persuaded to substitute for Edward Graziano.

At ten fifteen Goethe was to be at the Nobel Foundation, to pick up his cheque.

That Newton could not draw correct conclusions from all these false premises is self-evident. In his effort to convey the untruth and the impudence of his teaching, he had to deny everything a person, an observer and a thinker normally uses to convey his meaning: sense, sensual impression, commonsense and common usage of language.

(Goethe, *Theory of Colours,* quoted in Albrecht Schöne, *Goethes Farbentheologie,* C. H. Beck, page 37.)

———————

Something like the sun the eye must be,
Else it no glint of sun could ever see;
Surely God's own powers with us unite,
Else godly things would not compel delight.

(From Goethe's *Theory of Colours,* translated by Christopher Middleton, *Selected Poems,* John Calder, London 1983, page 127.)

chapter fifteen

For the silver-haired *Kriminalinspektör* Per Søderstrom, Friday, December 11 – a crisp, cold day with more snow in the offing – began splendidly. His stepdaughter Ulrike phoned at eight thirty – he had just arrived in his office on the fourth floor of the Bunker whose location cannot be revealed – and asked whether she could come and see him right away. She had something important to say. Søderstrom was very fond of her.

His secretary had put pink roses in the vase near the electronic black box on his desk. She had commiserated with him when he came in because it appeared to her inevitable that the causes of the medical laureate's sudden death would sooner or later be questioned. Søderstrom did not require commiseration for an event which had pumped more adrenaline into his system than anything that had happened since his appointment to his present position from that of senior lawyer in the Department of Forestry, and, before that, professor of computer science.

He had only three hours sleep and had already consumed at least one hour of news of last night's tragedy. Naturally, it saturated radio and television and the morning papers. From the moment of Edward Graziano's slide under the table at twenty minutes past seven last evening until the official announcement of his death six and a half hours later the *Kriminalinspektör* had been in constant touch with his colleagues in *Säpo*, the Swedish Security Service. (Their men had, of course, been on duty at the banquet.) For a long time every one in the police had expected that sooner or later a murder would be committed during the Nobel week.

Maybe a laureate would be the victim.

Or the murderer.

When the death of heart failure was announced, of course, the police had to assume that, until the contrary was proved, the real cause had been foul play – probably poisoning. Every police officer knew that if a death occurred under suspicious circumstances, the authorities would announce heart failure as the cause. Didn't everybody, sooner or later, die because the heart finally failed?

Starting immediately, Homicide and Security worked closely together accessing diverse databases that might yield useful information about the personnel of the Grand Hotel, particularly the kitchen personnel, on Robert Lovett, the personnel of the Nobel Foundation, of the Concert Hall and City Hall, including the two hundred volunteer waiters from all over Sweden, information about the escorts, and about the people attending the receptions Graziano had attended – including the hosts and hostesses – and about all those working at the other locations he had visited since his arrival, the University and research institutes. The systems used were primarily those described in Søderstrom's textbook *Computational Logic and Crime Detection,* SHU-YTW and ZORBA. At the same time the Swedish National Bureau, Interpol Stockholm, communicated with Interpol's General Secretariat in Lyon in southeast France to obtain information about Edward Graziano from Palo Alto, California, as well as from other places where he had been active. Interpol was also asked to obtain personal information about the other laureates, including Goethe. One of the *Säpo* agents had overheard a conversation at the luncheon at the German embassy on Tuesday, December 8, that Donald Heath was living in Toronto, Canada, with the wife of the deceased. So naturally there was special urgency in investigating Donald Heath's private life.

Søderstrom had called a short strategy meeting for nine o'clock. Those attending were *Polisinspektör* Knut Hansen from *Säpo, Polisintendent*Erik Martinsen from Criminal Intelligence, *Polisöverintendent* Carl Tilsen from Interpol Stockholm, a subdivision of the National Criminal Investigation Service, and Dr. Sven Nilsson from the *Statens Kriminaltekniska Laboratorium,* their most eminent expert on poisons.

Just after the meeting had adjourned, Ulrike arrived. She had taken a cab. Though she, too, had had very little sleep, she looked fresh, animated, pink faced, and, as usual, unkempt. Søderstrom already knew, of course, that his wife and daughter had met Goethe several times in Baden-Baden, and had become friends, and that Ulrike had persuaded Goethe to accept the Prize, even though at first he wanted to reject it. He also knew that his wife was exceptionally fond of Goethe. About two weeks ago, she even went as far as to say, during one of their many arguments, that she wouldn't hesitate to leave him and look after the Great Man if he invited her.

Søderstrom and Ulrike sat down at a little glass table near the window.

"So why are they saying 'heart failure'?" Ulrike asked.

"What about this," Søderstrom played with his golden pen. "Say, on Wednesday night Graziano had a minor heart attack, causing symptoms which frightened him because he was not familiar with them, not exactly heartburn, not exactly indigestion. He was a world-famous medical geneticist and knew something about the human body, and perhaps even, as a layman, about the human mind. Such knowledge does not exclude the possibility that he himself suffered from paranoia. Rather than believing he had a heart attack, he preferred to think he'd been poisoned by his enemies, rivals, competitors, whoever they were, perhaps by former students who thought he had mistreated them and who had a grudge against him. Maybe he'd been threatened and expected to be killed. Several hours later he suffered a massive attack and died soon afterwards. Is that not conceivable?"

"Perhaps." Ulrike was not very impressed. "Personally, I think it's a bit far-fetched."

"That we can only establish if you take me to Herr von Goethe so that I can ask him to confirm what you just told me. I would then ask the Karolinska for an autopsy. Do you happen to know where he is at the moment?"

She looked at her watch. Five to ten. "Probably having breakfast. At ten fifteen he has to be at the Nobel Foundation to pick up the cheque. But I don't think he's going to talk to you."

Søderstrom raised his eyebrows.

"What do you mean?"

Ulrike saw no reason for defending Goethe's position.

"He says he doesn't like the police."

"Why not?"

"He says it has something to do with growing up in a police state."

"Well, that's absurd."

"That's what I told him."

Søderstrom rubbed his chin.

"I think I will have to stage a little confrontation with the Great Man." He went over to his desk to look at his diary. "Let's go. I've got to be back here at eleven fifteen."

On 2.10.1808, while attending the Congress of Erfurt,
Napoleon summoned Goethe:
Goethe's audience with Napoleon lasted almost a whole hour.
I had accompanied him as far as the anteroom and waited
there till he came out.
The Emperor was sitting at a large round table having
breakfast, with Talleyrand standing on his right. He beckoned
Goethe to come nearer, and after looking at him closely asked
him how old he was. On learning that he was in his sixtieth
year he expressed his astonishment to find him still looking so
energetic, and passed immediately to the subject of Goethe's
tragedies. He also assured him that he had read The Sorrows
of Werther seven times and as evidence delivered an extremely
penetrating analysis of the novel.

(Friedrich von Müller, Chancellor at Weimar, quoted in *Goethe:*
Conversations and Encounters, edited by David Luke and Robert
Pick, Henry Regnery Company, Chicago 1966, page 71.)

chapter sixteen

Karen Svensen drove Goethe to the Nobel Foundation just after ten, to pick up the cheque. In the car he asked her, just to make conversation, whether it was true that Nobel Prizes could not be awarded posthumously.

"Yes, it is true. But I know why you're asking this," she said brightly. "You're wondering whether Graziano's estate would have been given the Prize money if he had died a few hours earlier, before the ceremony. Say, in the taxi, while you were talking to him. I happen to know the answer. According to Paragraph Four of the Statutes of the Nobel Foundation, Graziano's estate would have been given the money anyway because the Prize had been announced."

They were right on time. Karen Svensen promised to be back in fifteen minutes. The atmosphere was somber. Baron Gunnar Lennert greeted him, pale and bleary-eyed. The other laureates had already arrived. A bowl of chocolates was on a side table, wrapped in gold foil to look like Nobel gold medals. They had been generously provided by the candy manufacturer Alvin Bergholm.

Everyone thought, but nobody was saying, how lucky Donald Heath was. Unless Edward Graziano had changed his will, Heath's ménage was now enriched by the proceeds from two Nobel Prizes, his own and, thanks to his association with Graziano's widow Catherine, Graziano's. That meant twice $840,000 American, the equivalent of 6,700,000 Swedish kronor. In Canada, and probably everywhere else, this would be tax-free. In the United States it would be taxed.

The Baron distributed the envelopes containing the cheques. He then asked everyone to come to the library next door, please, for coffee. *Kriminalinspektör* Per Søderstrom was expected any moment. He had a few words to say to them.

So Ulrike had done what she said she would do, Goethe thought. And she might very well accompany her stepfather, too, to introduce him. And so far no minister had stopped the *Kriminalinspektör*.

He crossed the room to speak to Baron Gunnar Lennert.

"I'm afraid, Baron," he said. "I cannot stay. I promised to meet the French Ambassador at the hotel at eleven thirty."

"You would oblige me very much," the Baron replied in a surprisingly firm voice, "if you waited a few minutes. I'll ask my secretary to phone the Embassy. I'm sorry, but I'm afraid I have no choice."

Goethe considered for a second whether he should turn around and go anyway. The Baron would hardly dare to stop him physically. But of course his conciliatory side took over and he stayed.

They all went to the library and sat down on leather chairs around a table covered with learned journals and periodicals. A pretty young researcher named Maja Theolin entertained them with Nobel trivia.

"Did you know," she said, "that in 1922 Einstein didn't keep a single *pfennig*? He sent half of it to his first wife, Mileva, who very much needed the money. She may have done the necessary thinking for him in the first place, so he owed it to her. Anyhow, his second wife, Elsa, generously agreed. The other half of the money went to charities in Berlin. And did you know that Marie Curie used the money to instal a new bathroom in her house and then gave up teaching?"

At last Søderstrom arrived, with Ulrike at his side. Goethe had been right.

She went straight to Goethe to shake hands with him.

"My dear child," Goethe said to her in a low voice, "what mischief are you two up to."

"The *Kriminalinspektör* merely wants you to repeat to him what you said to me," Ulrike said.

"My dear, you know perfectly well that I won't speak to him."

Ulrike looked at him with an expression which made it clear to him that this was the moment when she finally decided she would not join him in Germany. She left the room.

The dark-blue pain gripped his abdomen. The last love affair of his life was over.

The Baron introduced every one individually. When his turn came

Goethe put on his *Mumiengesicht.*

"Herr von Goethe," Søderstrom said, "I hope you have a few minutes to spare for me after this short meeting."

"I'm afraid I do not, Officer."

Søderstrom smiled politely, walked to the other side of the room and leaned against the wall.

"Normally this should have been a time of rejoicing for you," he began. "And I'm sure what I have to say is the last thing you want to hear. Before I say it I must ask you with all the emphasis at my command to keep my remarks confidential. You will understand in a minute, why. We are all aware that officially the cause of Edward Graziano's death was heart failure. But in cases of sudden death of this nature, it has been our experience that it is wise to be prepared for all contingencies. There's now a definite indication that there may have been foul play. So far it has not been proved, but it is sufficiently substantial to demand an autopsy. It usually takes a little time to analyse the results and draw the necessary conclusions. Until this is done, you will understand that we cannot take any chances. Therefore, anybody, absolutely anybody who has been in contact with the deceased is automatically under suspicion. We must ask you to postpone your departure until this situation is resolved."

Hm, Goethe thought, not without amusement. Ulrike must have conveyed my views of the police to this gentleman. Now he's trying to punish me. Too bad my fellow laureates have to pay for my convictions.

Masao Okita was outraged.

"You mean we are under suspicion?" he asked.

"No more, and no less, than anybody else, Professor. "

His wife, Kanya, on the sidelines, found this a little difficult to accept.

"I would have thought that it would be a minimum courtesy, in any civilized country, to grant the laureates and their families immunity."

"I regret that you do not think Sweden is civilized," Søderstrom said with a quick little frown. "You will find that we will make sure, during the next few days, that you will not be restricted in your movements in any way. All we want is to make sure you don't leave the country. However, for the moment you may keep your passports."

"I will get in touch with my ambassador immediately, " Masao Okita said.

"Please do."

"I know your next line," Donald Heath said.

"What do you mean, Professor?"

"You're going to say 'I'm only doing my duty'."

"I was not going to say that," Søderstrom replied. "I would have thought that was obvious."

Elizabeth Priestley took a slightly different line from that of her colleagues.

"I think I'll confess right away, Inspector. I did it."

"In Sweden, Professor Priestley, we do not make jokes with the police."

"What a dull life you must lead, Inspector," Elizabeth Priestley said. "So, what are you going to do about it? I want to be arrested right away. And my husband wants me to be arrested, too. Don't you, dear?"

"Yes, dear. I do very badly," Ramsey Mansbridge agreed, lighting his pipe.

"I'm afraid we can't proceed just like that," Søderstrom said. "We will conduct a very comprehensive investigation before we arrest anybody."

"And how will you do that?" she asked.

"We have all the latest information technology," he replied.

"Oh, but think of all the time and effort you would save yourself if you just locked me up. Right now."

Søderstrom cut off the exchange.

"I don't want to waste any more of your time, ladies and gentlemen. Thank you very much."

He walked over to Goethe who stood up, ready to leave the room. Søderstrom blocked his way.

"You understand, of course, how reluctant we are to do this, Herr von Goethe," he said. "We are very much aware of your position in the world. I myself am a great admirer of your work. I have read your *Werther* at least twice, many years ago. Your young friend Miss von Levetzow told me about your conversation with the deceased yesterday, after the rehearsal in the Concert Hall. You will understand this matter is of vital importance to us. Would you mind giving me your account of this again, in your own words?"

"Yes, as I told you, Officer, I would mind. You will have to do your investigation without my help."

Goethe's lustrous, luminous, translucent brown eyes stared at Søderstrom with blood-curdling frigidity.

Without changing expression, Søderstrom unblocked the door and watched wordlessly as Goethe left the room.

Brander [in Auerbach's Tavern in Leipzig], singing:

There was a rat lived in the cellar, feeding on lard and butter.
Gave itself a tidy paunch and looked like Dr. Luther. The cook
put poison down for it. The poison griped and twisted it, like
love-pangs in the belly.

(Goethe, *Faust Part One,* Scene 5, translated by Barker Fairley,
University of Toronto Press 1970, page 32.)

chapter seventeen

By Sunday noon, December 13, Karl had received four documents containing some of the information he had asked for.

The first was the copy of a letter from Edward Graziano to Donald Heath. Saxco's agents had bribed the cleaning staff at Stanford University to look for relevant documents in Graziano's filing cabinet.

Palo Alto, California
December 2, 1992

Dear Donald Heath:

I cannot say I'm particularly looking forward to seeing you in Stockholm and I don't imagine that the sight of my face will throw you into fits of delight either. You were lucky to have been spared the sight of it since you left Stanford in August, taking my wife with you. Since then we have only communicated through lawyers. But a personal meeting in Stockholm is now unavoidable.

This is a threatening letter. Either Catherine returns to me before I leave for Stockholm or I will make your life hell on earth. I know about threatening letters because during the last few weeks I have received several myself. I know it's not always easy to decide whether one should be proud and brave and ignore them, or be realistic and sensible and prudent and pay attention to them. I only chose to be proud and brave because I could not give the letters to the police, for reasons which one day you will understand. My advice to you is to do what I would have done if I had been free to decide – be realistic, sensible and prudent.

Pay attention.

You are keeping Catherine against her will. There is nothing she, you or anybody else can say to change my mind about that. You may think of me whatever you want, but to her I am the only the man who counts. I've always encouraged her to have the odd fling with oversexed graduate students or even with stray Canadian professors like you who think they're God's comic gift to mankind. I've always found that once she's had her fill she appreciates me more. You see, Donald, she loves me. She loves the devil she knows. She also loves luxury. Plans are afoot to give her luxuries she never dreamed of, once she returns to me. She does not love you. I know her better than you do. *You're keeping her too long.*

If you don't give her her freedom before I depart for Stockholm, I will invest the eight-hundred-thousand-dollar Nobel Prize in making your life not worth living. I should have received the Nobel for my diabolical imagination, rather than for being a great benefactor to people with sore throats and sniffles. I will tell the world that you have stolen the research for your production of sonoluminescence and I will make this so plausible – please remember who I am – that no physics department in the Universe will ever touch you again. I will inform the press that you have awarded PhDs to your female students only on condition that they perform the most repulsively unnatural – no, bestial – acts with you in the lab. I will add that since you are famous for not having any sexual preference for women, that you did the same with boys. I will have sand poured into the tank of your Honda. I will make sure that the banks will no longer supply you with credit cards. I will have the Royal Canadian Mounted Police put you under surveillance because of your notoriously subversive politics. I will have you thrown out of every club you belong to. I will have sinister-looking men follow you on the street and I will make sure that your halitosis will be so disgusting that neither Catherine nor any other woman will ever want to consort with you again, even if you were able to...but you won't be because the necessary instrument will have withered on the vine. I will see to it that you stumble over a dead dog every night on your way home. I will arrange things so that no food will ever taste palatable again, and you will be chronically constipated, or the opposite. I will see to it that as soon as you think you've recovered from one attack of 'flu you'll get a new one. And if you escape with my wife to an island in the Caribbean, or to an igloo in the frozen north, the men and women I will hire to torture you will follow you there.

Be realistic, sensible and prudent.

I will see you in Stockholm,

Edward

———

A second document was found in Edward Graziano's office at Stanford University:
Dear Professor Graziano:
No one can guarantee your safety in Stockholm if you have the impudence to accept the Nobel Prize.

The signature was illegible

———

Saxco's agents in Stockholm found a letter in Elizabeth Priestley's and Ramooy Mansbridge's room in the Grand Hotel, written on hotel stationery.

Saturday, December 5, 1992

Dear Elizabeth:

I have reconsidered. I am extending the deadline until Thursday morning.

Edward

––––––––

The third document was a chapter on Edward Graziano from Elizabeth Priestley's unpublished memoirs. Saxco's operatives found it in London. According to the terms of her contract with the publisher, the book was to be published only after her death. It read:

Edward Graziano was one of the many gifted American graduate students in genetics who flocked to Cambridge in the 'fifties to work in the Cavendish Lab with Watson and Crick. Unlike most science students, he was an unrivaled conversationalist, on any subject under the sun. Edward was against everything. That was his specialty. There was not an idea anybody ever had over which he didn't pour cold water. But he did it with wit and charm, and it was evident that it was based on a kind of idealism, on the conviction that, if only we learned to think straight, the world would be a more honest place. I remember a French student once called him an American Voltaire. Edward said he wanted to be a founding member of the British Nihilist-Anarchist Party. All this was delightfully innocent compared to the sinister activities that were going on, so to speak, next door where Burgess and Maclean and others were being seduced for a very different cause. He often quoted a resolution of the Anarchist Parliament during the Spanish Civil War, to the effect that every woman had a moral, if not a legal obligation to satisfy the desire of any man she had aroused. He said that he was going to make that Paragraph One in the Manifesto of the British Nihilist-Anarchist Party, so he would at least get the entire male vote.

We lived on Richmond Terrace, just behind the Round Church. I will readily admit that, although I was sharing my digs with Jeremy, I found Edward immensely attractive. He certainly had a magnetic quality I found unique. This had a lot to do with concentration. When you were with him, no one else mattered. It was extraordinarily flattering. He made an immense effort to seem genuinely interested in everything about you and happily boasted that he had learned early in life that people, mainly women, liked nothing better than to talk about themselves. That is how he made his first conquest, he said, at the age of thirteen. By the time he was fourteen, he claimed, he could have any pretty woman he liked by just pretending to listen to her. His power of invention was unlimited. And he was hilarious. He let his women go on talking, he said, right through the act, while they were swinging from chandeliers, upside down, downside up, from left to right, right to left, during lectures, while writing exams, in Westminster Abbey, in the House of Commons, during garden parties on the grounds of Buckingham Palace. Often, when we met in our favourite pub, the Rose and Crown, he described his adventures in shockingly ungentlemanly detail. These were the 'fifties, after all, and we were all more shockable then than we are now. I never met any woman who actually had sex with him, though several, rather unconvincingly, claimed they had and gave him glowing reviews. He always made a determined effort to do it the way *they* liked, they said, and made them believe his own pleasure was the last thing he had in mind. He always joked he was a great human benefactor, that Cambridge couldn't do without him. He also boasted that if he didn't play devil's advocate, no one in Cambridge would ever have a bright idea. At that time we still had fun with him. Only in later years, when something within him snapped and he suddenly took himself seriously, did his humour turn into nasty, caustic, sadistic, destructive sarcasm.

I was not a virgin, far from it. Why then did I turn him down, again and again and again? Surely, since there was no evidence that any woman ever had sex with him, thousands of others must have turned him down as well. I never figured out why my rejection enraged him so much. I had no idea he would be so unforgiving. No doubt, if I had known that this was such a serious matter for him, I would have said, "All right, yes, why not? Saying yes is less time- and energy-consuming than saying no". After all, I'd had plenty of casual sex. There's no point in making a dangerous enemy over a little thing like that. But I stuck to my guns. I'm still trying to figure out why. True, I was living with Jeremy and I would have had to lie to him, but I lied to him about many more important things, so why not about this? Was I just being obstinate? Maybe I didn't want to do the obvious thing. Edward was certainly a more dynamic character than straightforward old Jeremy. But he was trying too hard. I never gave in.

In 1954 I was writing a dissertation on multiple epiphysial dysplasia (a group of skeletal disorders affecting bone formation resulting in dwarfism). Edward spent a lot of time in the lab as well, working on thalassemia. I had done a number of successful experiments with rats. Edward was always looking over my shoulder, giving me unsolicited advice. On a crucial day, I had to write up an experiment which I had not yet completed. I was in a rush to meet a deadline. Stupidly, I asked him what to do. He said, "You did it successfully last Tuesday, didn't you?" I said yes. I was sure I had, but I was wrong. "Well then, don't be a silly goose and go ahead and write it up." Later he said he did this deliberately because he knew I would be exposed as a cheat. He was trying to help, he added, because I was not cut out to be a geneticist. The dissertation was duly published. It was a tremendous success and launched me on what everybody, except Edward, predicted would be a glittering career in genetics. If I had been right it would have meant a decisive breakthrough. But somebody at Johns Hopkins tried to repeat the experiment and couldn't. Then others tried and couldn't. Then I tried and couldn't. I was summoned. I was forced to publish a correction. My career in genetics was finished.

I left Cambridge and switched to metallurgy and then to chemistry. I demonstrated the same talent for research I had shown in genetics. Twenty years passed. I never heard from Edward – no Christmas cards, nothing. But I was keeping track of him, and he of me. I got married – to Ramsey, not to Jeremy.

By 1974, I had a ten-year old daughter and was acquiring a certain reputation in Cambridge, not only as the cox during the Lent Headship races of the Lady Margaret Ladies Boat Club, which we won, but also in other respects, and so did Edward, at various American universities. He was not yet married. One day he was in London. He called me out of the blue and invited me to come down and have dinner with him at Bertorelli's on Charlotte Street. He had kept track of me, as I had of him. He was staying at a small hotel in Bloomsbury. I accepted. The dinner did not go particularly well. It was not exactly a disaster, but there were no sparks, and a few long stretches of silence. He didn't seem to be particularly interested in me, nor in any of our former friends. After dinner he wanted me to come back with him to his hotel. I declined. He did not insist.

Two weeks later a short letter arrived. It asked me, I thought rather peremptorily, and without any reference to our dinner, to arrange a scholarship at my college for one of his students. I wrote back and said I regretted but I could not oblige. He promptly sent me a registered letter and said if I did not get that scholarship within three weeks he would expose the fraud at the root of my career. I was an established researcher with a growing reputation and a Fellow of my College, but I did not yet feel sufficiently secure to be able deal with that. A taint, I thought, always leaves something unpleasant behind, especially since I could not deny the facts. So I yielded to the blackmail. Once I had yielded I had to yield again and again – I would guess more than a hundred times in the last twenty years. He made my life increasingly miserable. There was no end to his demands. I don't know how many jobs I had to get for his friends all over the world, how many grants, how many speaking engagements, how many prefaces and blurbs I had to write, how many conferences I had to organize. Then, in 1990, when my fifth book came out and I had received many awards, I decided I could at last afford to tell him to go to hell and say, "All right, go right ahead, tell the world about the horrible crime I committed forty years ago, I can take it". But he never did tell the world. He held back, he kept the matter in reserve, until the moment when both his and my Nobel were announced. Then he made his move. He first faxed me to say that I was going to hear from him shortly. I had expected it and, to be frank, I was afraid of it. Once he had spoken up, the Nobel Committee could not possibly go through with it and give me the Prize.

I pondered all kind of ways to stop him. It was a little late to offer him my body: I was in my late sixties. Still, I phoned him in California and asked him whether I could come and see him. He said, no thanks, he would prefer to communicate by letter or by fax. Then in mid-November he sent me his condition for keeping silent. I was to use the occasion of our getting the Nobel to persuade Her Majesty the Queen to become Patron of the

Elizabeth Priestley–Edward Graziano Fund, to be established on the occasion of our getting the Nobel. The Fund was to be devoted to educate the public to practice sexual abstinence in the interest of public health. In view of the current discussion on the future of the monarchy, caused largely by overindulgence in the royal family, Her Majesty would no doubt be delighted to agree. If I had not done so by December 5th, he would inform the Nobel Committee, etc., etc.

I did not meet his condition.

———————

The fourth document was found by Saxco's operatives in Tokyo. It was written in haste and sent with apologies that there had not been enough time to write it up properly.

Masao Okita is a cunning operator in High Finance. He has one foot in the University, the other in the Japanese Cabinet and is the brain behind the policy of investing in plants in East Asia: mainly disk drives in Singapore and memory chips in Korea. His wife is a left-wing lawyer and usually manages to shield him from any direct involvement in scandals. He and Kanya are joint owners of bars in the nightlife district of Kabukicho in Tokyo's Shinjuku Ward. At this moment the police are investigating a chain of homicides involving illegal immigration from China's southern provinces. Masao Okita's name has been mentioned in the proceedings. It is not clear in what connection. Okita is close to the Fuji-Bank. He is interested in the arts and backs traditional literary magazines. He shares a mistress named Raeka with Tatsuko Shimazu, the Minister of International Trade. His book on Taiwanese–Indonesian trade is on every academic reading list. He predicts a Japanese trading surplus with the rest of the world of one trillion dollars by the year 2000 and is convinced Japanese non-democratic neo-capitalist oligarchies will supersede U.S. as the world's dominant society.

There is an indirect connection with Edward Graziano. Okita is chairman of the board of the Yamura Institute. They do biotech research and have a productive and ambitious rhinovirus division. Okita invested millions in the Institute on condition they make his old friend Kunei Kido the director. The father of Kido and the father of Okita were both prominent after 1945, in various revolutionary movements. In opposition to their fathers, both Kido and Okita are traditional. Their intimate friend was the late celebrity writer Yukio Mishima, the famous aesthete of death and fighter against vulgarizing and trivializing genuine Japan who committed *hara-kiri* in 1970.

In their research, Kido and Graziano were deadly rivals. Each had spies in the other's labs. Last spring Graziano was convinced Kido was ahead. So he indirectly conveyed to leading medical geneticists around the world a summary of an imaginary forthcoming article in *Science*, pointing out fatal flaws in Kido's research that he invented. These communications could not easily be traced to him. The purpose was to throw Kido's team off balance. The ploy was totally successful. Graziano made his breakthrough while Kido's people were trying to recover. In October, Graziano's Nobel Prize was announced. A day later, in shame over his loss, Kunei Kido committed *hara-kiri* in Yamura Institute's picturesque garden, in front of witnesses. He drew a short blade across his midriff from left to right. The *coup de grâce* was performed by Masao Okita, his *kaishaku,* by neatly decapitating him with a heavy, two-handed sword.

Also, am I not learning when at the shape of her bosom,
Graceful lines, I can glance, guide a light hand down her hips?
Only thus I appreciate marble; reflecting, comparing,
See with an eye that can feel, feel with a hand that can see.
True, the loved one besides may claim a few hours of the daytime,
But in night hours as well makes full amends for the loss.
For not always we're kissing, often hold sensible converse;
When she succumbs to sleep, pondering, long I lie still.
Often too in her arms I've lain composing a poem,
gently with fingering hand count the hexameter's beat.

(Goethe, Roman Elegies, Number 6, translated by Michael Hamburger,Selected Poems, edited by Christopher Middleton, John Calder, London 1983, page 107.)

———————

In other times, Goethe continued, I had a completely different experience in relation to my poems. Beforehand I had no impression of them, and no concept. They suddenly overwhelmed me and insisted on being created immediately, so that instinct propelled me to write them down, as though in a dream. It often happened that in such a somnabulistic state I had a lopsided piece of paper in front of me, a fact I only noticed when I had covered the page and could not find any more space on it to continue. I used to keep several of such written pages, but over time I seem to have lost them.

(J. P. Eckermann, *Gespräche mit Goethe*, F. A. Brockhaus Wiesbaden 1959, March 14, 1830, page 549.)

chapter eighteen

The time had not yet come when Goethe would be able to cope with his anguish over Ulrike's rejection of him. To survive it emotionally so that he could write *Faust Part Two,* he would have to find an appropriate method of self-help, not quite as easy at his age as it used to be. In the meantime, he had to win the race with Søderstrom's computers. The communications Karl had received clearly established convincing, but not yet compelling, motives for three laureates to poison Edward Graziano, certainly a promising beginning. But there was still a great deal of work to do. For him to win the race, he had to summon his inner voices.

———

Lucia was a Sicilian saint who lived in the fourth century A.D. So far no one has been able to find out how she became part of the Christmas celebrations in Sweden, and not in Denmark, not in Norway, nor even in Italy. She was burned at the stake, for some reason, and her eyes were plucked out, presumably under her original name, which is unknown. Posthumously, through a process of inverse logic, she was given the name Lucia because it was derived from the Latin *lux.* The light was taken out of her eyes.

In the old Julian calendar, December 13th, Saint Lucia Day, was the shortest day – and the longest night – of the year. In every Swedish home in the early morning of December 13th, a procession celebrates the saint who brings light to the longest Swedish night. The oldest daughter of the family, wearing flickering candles on her head and carrying a plate of cookies, with several others accompanying her, does the rounds singing *Santa Lucia*. If there are sons, they wear golden stars on their heads and are known as star boys. No Christmas would be complete without Lucia.

This was the kind of custom Goethe liked. He was looking forward to the visitation which, as Karl had explained to him, was provided by the hotel. The Nobel Foundation was paying for it.

Early on Sunday morning, when he was fully awake, he rose, went to the door and unlocked it. When the little saint and her companions would knock, all he had to do was to say "Come in!" Karl had told him that in 1976, Goethe's predecessor, Saul Bellow, who had not been warned, opened the door stark naked. The visiting saint and her companions were allowed, no doubt for the first time in their lives, but not necessarily for the only time, to obtain a full view of a winner of the Literature Prize *in natura*.

After unlocking the door Goethe returned to his bed to continue his meditations, decently covered by a duvet.

There was a knock at the door. The Saint Lucia procession had arrived.

"Come in!"

A blond saint, singing *Santa Lucia* a little out of tune, came in. Goethe recognized her immediately. It was Robert Lovett's enchanting companion, the nymphet he brought to the rehearsal at the Concert Hall, the lovely Lolita who was enjoying her first puberty. Her breasts under the white gown with the silver sash were two delicious little rosebuds. Goethe noticed with a shiver of delight the unmistakable symptoms of sexual arousal.

Lolita's three companions, two boys and a girl, were a year or two younger. They carried plates of cookies. Five candles were flickering on her head. There could be no question that she knew who he was. But should he make it known to her that he recognized her?

Then something extraordinary happened.

The saint came close to Goethe's bed and, still singing, looked him in the eye, smiling, so provocatively impudent that Goethe jumped out of bed, took off her wreath of flickering candles so as not to start a catastrophic hotel fire, and kissed her firmly on that insolent mouth. She threw her arms around him and kissed him back.

Her three companions laughed and said something incomprehensible, clearly indicating amused approval.

Goethe said, "Thank you, my child," took a cookie from the plate, went back to bed and covered himself again with his duvet.

Lolita said, "Thank *you*, Herr von Goethe, and now, would you please write something in my book."

She pulled a little notebook from inside her shirt-front and handed it to him.

He wrote, munching the cookie, without a moment's thought:

If I were a painter you would be a little angel in everyone of my pictures. [2]

———

After they left he looked at his watch. It was only half past seven. He could stay in bed for another hour, before meeting Karl for breakfast downstairs at nine. There was enough time for him to doze off again.

It was during that hour that Goethe, half-asleep, summoning his inner voices and savouring that kiss, solved the crime.

The process began with a meditation on the kiss.

It was not, by any means, an innocent kiss, he thought. But what, in relation to kisses, was innocent and what was not? Did that delightful shiver of delight marking his arousal under the duvet turn innocence into something else? If ever evidence was required for the intricacy of mind–body relations, that involuntary arousal was more than enough. Surely innocence was a moral concept. If it was involuntary, how could it have been immoral? He certainly felt the itch of desire, moral or immoral, and desire always had a target. He was still feeling it now, very much, a desire very different from the feelings he had for Ulrike which went beyond the physical and had a different target. This desire was not satisfied by the kiss, however pleasurable the experience. Obviously it would never be satisfied. Fortunately it was a most fruitful aspect of human desire that it was rarely satisfied. The art of living consisted of capitalizing on this and using unsatisfied desire to keep the Universe going – and to solve murders. Satisfied desire was useless.

And what kind of desire, if any, did the girl experience? Was her kiss innocent? Judging from the way she used her tongue, by no means. No doubt in Swedish sex education classes the word innocence was unknown. But how did they handle desire?

Who was she? Surely her employment as Saint Lucia by the management of the Grand Hotel and her role as companion of Robert Lovett was coincidental. But wasn't it a curious coincidence? Was the

---

[2] "Wär ich ein Maler du solltest als Engelchen überall sein." *Goethe's Selected Poems,* edited by Christopher Middleton, John Calder, London 1983, page 37.

finger of Fate pointing at something? Was she an agent of Søderstrom, instructed to visit all the laureates and their retinues in their hotel rooms to find out who was with whom? No, that was absurd.

Goethe reconstructed the scene he saw at the beginning of the rehearsal on Thursday. Lovett handed Graziano an envelope, Graziano tore it open, glanced at what was inside it, rose in a huff, and sat down close to the stage.

That was it. Lovett was the murderer. There was open hatred, open war, between Lovett and Graziano. Didn't Graziano say he was used to death threats? Well, the letter in the envelope was a death threat. When Graziano told him in the taxi he knew who had poisoned him, and why, Lovett was the person he meant.

And what did the girl have to do with any of this?

Nothing.

Goethe had won the race for humanity. He picked up the pad of paper he always had on his night table and wrote down "Robert Lovett. Eight fifteen a.m., December 13th." All that was needed now was evidence of a motive. Inexorably, the proof would follow.

At breakfast Karl handed Goethe a second report from Tokyo.

Twelve years ago, Robert Lovett was a gifted graduate student of Professor Edward Graziano at Stanford University. He was suffering from severe and protracted depressions which forced him to drop out of the University. Lovett's departure greatly disappointed the professor. He had established an excellent relationship with him, as he occasionally did with promising students.

Lovett was the only son and heir of the late meat-packing magnate Harry Lovett, of Lovett and Greenshields in San Francisco. Soon after Lovett had left the University he made an arrangement with Graziano according to which Graziano would make available to him the genetically engineered anti-depressant drug MNY-114, which was not yet on the market. He could not promise it, but there was a good chance it would, combined with psychotherapy, restore Lovett's mental health, revive his energy and sense of well-being and enable him to resume his studies. The drug had not yet been approved by the Food and Drug Administration and was highly addictive, but Graziano assured him that it was, as far as he could tell, exactly what Lovett needed. Only he, Graziano, could provide it, through his connections.

He spelled this out carefully and this made Lovett dependent on him while the addiction lasted. Lovett would not only be able to continue his academic work but Graziano would also be glad to include him in his rhinovirus research team. If the drug was as effective, as he was sure it would be, Lovett would, by a given day, transfer to Graziano fifteen million dollars, required for the research program.

The drug proved to be effective, just as Graziano had indicated it would be, and Lovett gladly complied with the financial clauses of the contract. In fact, the arrangement worked perfectly. The two men complemented each other's talents splendidly and became close friends. The result of their cooperation was the Nobel Prize to Graziano "for his discovery of new possibilities in understanding the mutation of rhinoviruses by means of genetic manipulation." He invited Lovett, who was by then his senior researcher, to accompany him to Stockholm for the ceremonies. This was a particularly welcome invitation since Lovett, who was unmarried, had a sister in Stockholm, who was married to a Swedish businessman and had a daughter. Lovett was very fond of his niece.

But there were dark thunder clouds on the horizon.

Last spring, Graziano launched a new phase of the research. He begun assembling a second team, using only three members of the first team. One of these was Robert Lovett. There was a radical change in the atmosphere. Graziano suddenly became secretive and uncommunicative and repeatedly rebuffed Lovett when he requested information. It soon became evident to Lovett and others that something sinister was going on. If he had not still been dependent on Graziano for the anti-depressant drug MNY-114, he would have broken off relations at that time. To take care of any contingency, he took steps – eventually successful steps which cost him many thousands of dollars – to locate alternative sources of the still unapproved medication.

In September, there was a tense confrontation between the two men. Graziano told him an amazing story, hoping against hope that, because of Lovett's dependency on him, he would remain loyal. He said he had been asked by agents of the government of Iraq to modify the rhinovirus virus into a bubonic plague virus in return for a considerable portion of whatever oil revenues Iraq was earning after the Gulf War, legally or illegally. Saddam Hussein knew there was only one genetic engineer in the whole world who could provide him with these germs. Graziano was convinced that fabulous wealth would induce Catherine to return to him. If Lovett leaked this story, Graziano said, to the police or anybody else, there were many means available to him "to take care" of him swiftly, and, for Graziano, safely.

Lovett kept the secret, having decided to "take out" Graziano, and to do it in Sweden rather than California, under such circumstances and in such a manner that even the greatest pathologists in the world would establish the cause of death unmistakably as heart failure.

Others leaked parts of the secret. Hence, Graziano received a number of death-threatening letters. But, strangely enough, as far as anybody could tell as yet, no communication was sent to the Nobel Foundation.

Faust: You beast. You foul monster. O infinite spirit, turn this reptile back into its canine form, the dog, that used to run ahead of me on my evening walks, roll at the feet of unsuspecting strangers and jumped on their shoulders when they tripped over him. Turn him back into the shape that suited him so that he may crawl again in the sand at my feet, him the lowest of the low.

(*Faust Part One,* Scene 23, Scene 26, translated by Barker Fairley, University of Toronto Press 1970, page 77.)

chapter nineteen

O n Tuesday morning the pathologist Dr. Sven Petersen of the Karolinska Hospital phoned Per Søderstrom. Later in the day, he faxed him the autopsy report.

"There's one thing I thought I should tell you before you read it," he said. "This was a very unusual case. The deceased could easily have died of heart disease, just as had been thought originally. I would assess the chances that the true cause of death would be discovered at one thousand to one. You see, at the point where the left coronary artery bifurcates into the anterior descending–"

"Dr. Petersen," Søderstrom stopped him, "you need not go on. I prefer to read the report later. What, in short, was the cause of death?"

"That is what I wanted to tell you, *Kriminalinspektör.* A careful toxicological examination of the blood demonstrated beyond doubt that the cause of death was the substance Monolit, which entered his system about fifteen hours before death occurred."

―――――

A vial of Monolit was found in Robert Lovett's shaving kit. It was a genetically engineered substance related to rhinoviruses.

―――――

Excerpts from the Press Conference Kriminalinspektör Per Søderstrom held in his office on Tuesday afternoon, December 15, 1992, at three p.m.

Q. We understand Robert Lovett has been arrested. Has he made a statement?

A. The American Embassy made a lawyer available to the suspect. In the meantime Mr. Lovett has been instructed not to say anything to anybody.

Q. Can you tell us how the poison was administered?

A. I can. It appears that the suspect managed to steal the key-card from Professor Graziano, then used it during the night from Wednesday to Thursday to enter his room while the deceased was asleep and cover his toothbrush with a toxic substance. In the morning, when Professor Graziano used it, he recognized it immediately by its distinctive taste. As a medical man he understood that once that particular poison had entered his system, even if only by mouth, it was too late to save him. He therefore knew he had only a few hours to live. His life had been threatened several times prior to his arrival in Stockholm and at least once in Stockholm. So he was prepared. The most important thing for him, under the circumstances, was to remain alive until he had received the Nobel Prize. And this he did.

Q. Are you concerned that this murder may have inflicted irreparable damage to Sweden's reputation?

A. Of course. But the public understands that even the best police force in the world cannot provide absolute protection against a determined criminal.

Q. What was it that alerted you first to the possibility of foul play?

A. A call from my stepdaughter on Friday morning. She is acquainted with Goethe. She told me about a significant conversation Goethe had with the deceased shortly after noon on Thursday. It is entirely due to Goethe's alerting her to the murder that the crime has been solved. Our investigation led to the suspect with great speed. Thanks to our informatics, and with the encouragement and full support of the highest levels of government, we had little difficulty in following up the lead. Particular thanks are due *Polisinspektör* Knut Hansen from *Säpo* for his work on fingerprints, to *Polisintendent* Erik Martinsen from Criminal Intelligence for his electronic analysis of food and drink and for his computer studies of hotel key-cards, to *Polisöverintendent* Carl Tilsen from Interpol Stockholm for archival searches in California, Japan and the U.K., and the Nobel Foundation right here, and to Dr. Sven Nilsson from the *Statens Kriminaltekniska Laboratorium* for his highly sophisticated chemical studies, using some new analytical techniques for the first time. Thanks are also due to the management of the Grand Hotel for their devotion to patriotic duty in cooperating with us. Thanks to all these we had solved the case by eight fifteen in the morning of December 13th.

Had my stepdaughter not called me I would undoubtedly have accepted the official announcement from the Karolinska Hospital whose integrity has never been questioned. I personally take exception to certain speculation in foreign newspapers that the original intention of our authorities had been to suppress the truth.

To Johann Wolfgang von Goethe, to this Great Man, to this Universal Sage, to this Olympian, must go the full credit for the successful investigation. In the name of the Swedish people, I herewith express to him our deepest gratitude.

chapter twenty

Immediately after his press conference, Per Søderstrom had to fly to Seattle to attend a conference of criminologists organized by Microsoft. This made it possible for Karl to spend his last night in Stockholm, the night from Tuesday to Wednesday, taking her husband's place at Amalie's side in their villa in the Djurgården, the Deer Garden. She asked Karl to take special care not to leave his shaving things in the bathroom so that Ulrike's two younger sisters would not ask any unnecessary questions.

The question uppermost in Amalie's mind was whether the events of the week had enhanced or lessened her chances to join Goethe to sweeten his remaining years.

"I wish," she said while Karl was smoking his post-coital cigarette, "Ulrike wasn't such a goody-goody. Why should she ruin her chances to spend a little time with Goethe only because she didn't like his attitude to my husband? I don't blame Goethe for not liking Per. I wish she wasn't so fond of him."

"I can't make her out at all," Karl yawned. "She's your daughter, not mine."

"I mean," Amalie continued, "it was such a good idea. It would have done her so much good. But I'm afraid Goethe would have become bored with her very quickly."

By now Karl was half asleep. He grunted.

"I was pleased that Per said such nice things about Goethe. That was very generous of him, after the way Goethe treated him. Do you know why he did that?"

Karl made a snoring sound.

"Because I asked him to."

By now he was fast asleep.

———————

It was clear to Goethe that he would never be able to write *Faust Part Two* unless he found a way immediately, that very afternoon, in Karl's jet while flying back to Frankfurt, to translate his anguish over the loss of Ulrike into a play, a film script or a poem. No other catharsis, no other self-help had ever worked for him. In the meantime, he would play his part as a benign public celebrity in the last phase of his Nobel Week.

Lovett was arrested on Tuesday morning. At that moment, when at last the laureates were free to go home, their high spirits returned. They knew that sooner or later they would find out what had motivated Lovett, and they did not have to waste time thinking about it now. On Wednesday morning they were assembling in the lobby, with their suitcases containing their gold medals, to say goodbye to Baron Gunnar Lennert and to the various dignitaries who had entertained them throughout the week. Amalie and Ulrike also arrived. They called Goethe in his room. At last he came down, wearing his maroon turtleneck sweater and grey slacks. His mood seemed serene.

The laureates lined up to shake hands with him.

"What I always forgot to ask you," he said to Masao Okita and his bird-like wife, "was did you by any chance know my old friend Yukio Mishima?"

"But of course," Okita replied, delighted with the question.

"Then you must also have known Kunao Kido."

Kido was the geneticist whose *kaishaku,* decapitation, Masao Okita had neatly performed with a two-handed sword as a result of Graziano being awarded the Nobel Prize.

Okita opened his mouth in speechless astonishment at Goethe's reference to his dead friend.

His petite, sharp-witted wife, Kanya, professor of anthropology in Kyoto, came to his rescue.

"You must write a play about Kido," she said. "Then you will understand the side of Japan that's not usually covered in the press releases."

For Elizabeth Priestley and the pipe-smoking Ramsey Mansbridge,

Goethe had a similarly pointed remark.

"Why don't you write your memoirs, Elizabeth," he said as he kissed her wrinkled cheek.

"But I already have," she replied.

"So why have they been withheld from me?" he asked indignantly.

"Because they're not to be published until I've departed."

"She doesn't want any trouble with all her old boyfriends, you know," Ramsey Mansbridge volunteered.

"Well," Goethe smiled, "One of them has just been dealt with."

"What do you mean?" Elizabeth cried.

"I have eyes in my head," Goethe declared. "I have been watching you all week. And him, while he was still with us."

The farewell from Donald Heath ran along different lines. With his comedian's face, unkempt curly hair and sparkling eyes, he seemed in top form.

"Ah, Professor Sonoluminescence," Goethe said, "the man who's devised a system to produce light from sound, you must invite me to visit you in your frozen country. I want to recite for you the full text of a poem that illustrates your thesis perfectly."

"You mean you wrote one for me?"

"No, my friend, not yet. It's by Dylan Thomas and it's called *From Love's First Fever to her Plague*. Do you know it?"

"Afraid not."

Goethe began reciting in his beautiful baritone.

"And the four winds, that had long blown as one,
Shone in my ears the light of sound
Called in my eyes the sound of light...

"Shall I go on?"

"Let's wait till you come to Toronto. Nothing would please us more."

"Us? You mean you and your...beautiful companion? I have heard a good deal about her. "

"You have? From whom?"

"We poets live on inspiration. Therefore we're unable to disclose our sources."

Heath lowered his voice.

"Did *he* mention me in his conversation with you?"

"No," Goethe assured him. "He did not. I assume it would not have been flattering."

"No, it definitely would not." He raised his voice again. "Back to your coming visit to Canada. It will be a major event, from coast to coast. I can see the headlines – 'Goethe in Canada.' The schools will be closed. Kids will line the streets while you wave to them from behind a glass cage in the open stretch-limousine. We used to adore royal visits but I'm afraid they've gone out of fashion."

The last to say goodbye were Amalie and Ulrike.

"I shall visit you soon," Amalie said.

Goethe bowed, gallant as ever. "That would give me immense pleasure."

"Goodbye, Wolfgang," Ulrike kissed him on the forehead.

"Goodbye, my child."

"And thank you so much," these were Amalie's last words, for the moment, "for being so kind to Ulrike."

On September 5, 1823, a post-chaise was being driven along the highway from Carlsbad to Eger...None of the company uttered a word, for since leaving Carlsbad, where young women and girls bade the old man farewell with loving looks and kisses, Goethe had not once opened his lips in speech. He lolled back in the carriage, musing; but his face showed that he was inwardly stirred. At the first halt he alighted, and his two companions saw him scribble something on a piece of paper. The same thing happened each time the horses were changed on the journey to Weimar. Hardly did they set foot in Hartenberg Castle, the second day of the journey, when he started to write down what had been shaping itself in his mind during the drive; thus it happened in Eger, and again in Pössneck. His diary merely tells laconically: "Worked at the poem" (September 6); "Sunday, went on writing the poem" (September 7); "Again went through the poem" (September 12). At Weimar, the work was finished. It was no less a poem than the "Elegy" in his Trilogy of Passion, the most significant, most intimate, and therefore the most cherished poem of his old age; it was a heroic farewell, and marked a heroic new departure.

Stefan Zweig, The Marienbad Elegy, *The Tide of Fortune,* The Viking Press, New York 1940, page 167.

Ulrike von Levetzow was nearly a hundred when she died in 1899. She had spent her life in the Convent Zum Heiligen Grabe. A friend of hers recorded a conversation with her in old age.
"I knew that the pretty and wealthy Fräulein von Levetzow had had many suitors, and I once told her that I was surprised that she had never married.
"'I was loved by Goethe,' she replied, with a proud and bittersweet smile.

"Whenever a man approached her since then, she said, she missed something in him. They all left her cold. She was too young at the time to become herself inflamed by the passion she had aroused and realized only later that no man would ever be able to offer her the kind of glow she had kindled in Goethe. So she turned down one suitor after another.
"'I would have been too bored with them,' she said."

(From *Goethe Erzählt Sein Leben,* Fischer Taschenbuch 5600, Fischer Taschenbuch Verlag GMBH, Frankfurt am Main 1982, page 489.)

Part Three

FAUST PART TWO

From *Zeitgeist*, Berlin, December 13, 2002
An essay by Kurt Schmidt

Goethe occasionally called his entire literary output "One Great Confession". Earlier this year, in the tributes following his death on March 22, many were wondering what it was he was confessing in *Faust Part Two*, which has just been published.

It is an open question whether we will see it on the stage in the foreseeable future, although there is not a major theatre in the world, from Rio to Tokyo, that has not put in a bid for the rights. It will be incredibly hard to produce. The delay does not worry me in the least. For me, what matters is the language and the intellectual content, and I can enjoy these perfectly well in print. I can wait for a few decades before I see it on the stage, on film or on television. Extravagant multimedia effects, music and dancing will have to make up for the lack of dramatic tension. It is an epic in verse rather than a drama, a novel à la Don Quixote or Ulysses rather than a play like Hamlet, a road movie rather than a sitcom. Faust continues his restless journey, constantly striving and constantly straying. He is always in search of excitement, intellectual and sensual, always conscious, however dimly, of the right path, relentlessly trying to understand "what keeps the world together in its innermost core." He is not Everyman but an exceptionally gifted individual, like the author himself, who experiences the world. It is not his personality but the story of his life that is designed to be symbolic of the life of humanity.

After the release of Goethe's film *Elegy*, a few months after he received the Nobel Prize in 1992, nine years ago, the public knew that the part of the young student Lili who was so beautifully acted by Marianne Linsberger was modeled on Ulrike, the daughter of an old friend whom Goethe had met some years earlier in Baden-Baden. In this deeply moving, clearly autobiographical film the old magician created – he even used the word "manufactured" – his love in order to complete his life's work, without any real expectation that she would return it. Subconsciously, he had known all along that he would have to renounce her. Now, with the appearance of *Faust Part Two*, we know that Goethe's last love has served its purpose. *Elegy* was indeed a true confession.

But what about *Faust Part Two*? What was he confessing? That is a difficult question. One could see that in *Faust Part One* he confessed that in order to fulfil himself as a poet and scientist he made others suffer. But how can a poem about human existence, as such, be a personal confession? Only if we think of a confession as meaning an outpouring of ideas and impressions, absolutely true to life and full of contradictions, loose ends, fairy tales, mythological "jests", Jungian allegories, riddles and codes.

It is futile, for example, to ask who won the bet – Faust or Mephisto. Both did. Ambiguity pervades the work. There is only one thing that is beyond irony – God's love and mercy. Everything else, including human justice, is cast in doubt. Goethe actually had Gretchen welcome Faust's Factor X in the Beyond – the same Gretchen whose mother and brother he had killed, and for whose death and that of their child none other than Faust was responsible. There, in the Beyond, Faust's Factor X was put to work in an atmosphere of everlasting erotic bliss. What else could the already famous line about the Eternal Feminine mean? No wonder Mephisto protested that there was no justice for him, neither human nor divine. Surely he was right to complain that there was nobody to appeal to. Our hearts go out to the devil.

Goethe did not wish to have the play published until after his death. The world, he said when he sealed the manuscript a few weeks before he died, was too confused to be able to deal with it, even his "valued friends" were not to read it while he was alive. To one of his old admirers he wrote that he had sealed it with some regret because he hated to deprive him and other intimates of some hours of fun – he used the word *Spass* (fun), not *Vergnügen* (pleasure) – which his seriously intentioned *Scherze* (jests) might have given them. He actually presented *Faust Part Two* as a *scherzo*. (The Italians borrowed *Scherz* from the Germans to coin *scherzare*. This led to *scherzo*, possibly via the Germanic language of Longobardic – one of the few instances when the Italians acquired a light touch from the Germans.) Goethe added that his friends would have been amused by some of the thoughts that had been percolating in his mind for the last few years. Also, he did not wish to be irritated by critics telling him they couldn't understand it. He knew they would never grasp that a play about human existence could be true without being clear. He must have enjoyed playing his last game – to outmanoeuvre death, to live beyond the grave.

As the play opens, Faust has only superficially recovered from the Gretchen trauma, by the simple process of forgetting, a process much helped by sleep. Now it is time to wake up and resume his journey, in Goethe's words, "to strive and strive to reach the summit of existence." Whenever possible, Goethe satirizes his old enemy, that soulless scientist, Lili's stepfather. This time it is Dr. Wagner, the geneticist who inherited Faust's laboratory where he happens to be engineering a test-tube baby. In one scene he gives Mephisto a lecture on what has been learned about DNA since his old professor and mentor, Dr. Johannes Faust, made his original, unpublished discoveries:

"We now know a good deal more about genes than we did before Professor Dr. Faust made his discoveries. We've learned that they contain long strings of digital information, just like computers and CDs. But the genetic code is not a binary code as in computers, nor an eight-level code as in some telephone systems, but a quaternary code, with four symbols."

Dr. Wagner's creation is Homunculus, a name Goethe borrowed from alchemy, meaning artificial man. Playing his usual games with mind–body relations, Goethe made Homunculus a sexless human psyche, a kind of Factor X, rather than a complete specimen of homo (or femina) sapiens. Homunculus is pure brain power, sexless in spite of its male name, pure spirit inhabiting a tiny body, a device for Goethe to make fun of the pure, unrelieved, unadulterated intellectual life. (In his film *Elegy*, Goethe's alter ego advised Lili to go skiing in the Dolomites, rather than write her essays.) It will be Homunculus's job to lead Faust to Helena, the Gretchen of *Part Two*.

In one scene Homunculus wakes up Faust and speaks to him directly in his high-pitched, sexless, impudent voice.

"My dear Faust," Homunculus says, "I know what you were

dreaming. You had a sex dream. You were" – here he uses a vulgar word, to demonstrate his humanity – "Helena. Am I right?"

Faust rubs his eyes and stretches his limbs.

"Yes, you're right."

"Do you want to do it when you're awake?"

"I do."

"I will take you to her."

But it is Mephisto, not Homunculus, whom Faust first asks to take him to Helena.

"All right." Mephisto says after some hesitation. "I hate to reveal to you one of our Higher Secrets. But there it is. You'll first have to visit The Mothers. I assure you it's not much fun."

"The Mothers?"

"I know the idea gives you the shivers. The Mothers are goddesses throned in solitude, outside of place, outside of time, unknown to mortal beings. You'll have to dig deep to reach them."

"Show me the way."

"There is no way. You'll enter the untrodden, the untreadable, the unpermitted, the unpermissible. Are you ready? There are no doors, no locks, no bolts. You'll be pushed about from one emptiness to another. Do you know what emptiness is?"

"In this emptiness of yours," Faust shoots back, "I will find everything."

"I hope you know what you're doing. Here is the key."

"Just a second. I thought you said there were no doors, no locks, no bolts."

"Take it."

"That little thing?"

"Don't underestimate it!"

"Look! It's growing in my hand. It's shining, flashing!"

"At last you're beginning to understand! Now let your nature will your descent. Stamp your foot and you'll go down. Stamp again and you'll come up."

Faust stamps his foot and disappears.

Mephisto, to the audience: "I wonder whether he'll ever come up again."

When Goethe conceived this scene he closely followed Jung's passages in *Symbols of Transformation,* written as early as 1912. The key, of course, is the libido, which is "not only creative but recreative, and also possesses an intuitive faculty, a strange power 'to smell the right place', almost as if it were a live creature with an independent mind of its own." In *Faust Part One,* the libido was primarily the sexual urge. But in *Part Two,* it is something even more powerful, "a force of nature, good and bad at once, or morally neutral," as Jung put it. And when Goethe discussed his plans with Jung, Jung said, "Your man Faust will need his phallic wand in order to bring off the greatest wonder of all – the creation of Helena. The insignificant-looking tool in Faust's hand is the dark creative power of the Unconscious which reveals itself to those who follow its dictates and indeed is capable of working miracles."

Goethe cannot show us the unshowable – what happens in the realm of The Mothers, how Helena was created. But he does show us the result, at the Emperor's court in cyberspace, with Faust and Mephisto in attendance. Out of nowhere, suddenly, a holograph of his creation, of the virtual Helena, appears. She is Goethe's greatest *Scherz,* bringing the Helena of Greek mythology, and of Johann Spiess's and Christopher Marlowe's *Doctor Faustus,* into the twenty-first century.

"Do I see with my eyes?" Faust exclaims. "Or is it deep in my inner mind that the source of beauty is thus poured out before me? My fearful journey has brought a marvellous reward. How futile the world was, before it was opened to me...To you I owe the spring of every action, and the quintessence of passion."

It is the speech which, in Marlowe's version, read "Was this the face that launched a thousand ships?"

"Pull yourself together!" Mephisto snaps at him.

But it is too late. Faust has reached out for her. There is an explosion – clouds of smoke darken the stage. Faust collapses. Mephisto throws Faust over his shoulder and walks off.

Jung's comment, when Goethe told him about his plans years ago, was "That's exactly right, Wolfgang. Faust's greedy attempt to take possession of an archetypal figure has to explode the situation and a regression is bound to follow."

––––––––––

The Great Confession, I repeat, is the news that love conquers all. What a relief! We all thought the important thing was to strive rather than to love. Loving is definitely more pleasant and easier and its rewards more evident. But did Goethe really mean it? He would say that only pedants like Lili's stepfather are consistent. The apparent downgrading of the work ethic implicit in this Great Confession, which for so many years was said to be at the core of Goethe's message, was intimately related to another shocker – his anti-egalitarian belief that what weighs most heavily in the scale of things was Personality, that it was more important *to be* somebody, rather than *to do* something. But in order to be somebody in Goethe's eyes one had to be constantly and restlessly striving. The angels who carry Faust's Factor X to Gretchen's care in Heaven sing that "anybody who keeps striving can be redeemed" from evil and from the devil.

And what about the cult of restlessness, the very core of the Faust–Mephisto wager? What about the strange notion that if Faust stopped for (an almost) Perfect Moment on his journey, to admire a girl or a landscape – "oh stop, let me linger for a moment" – he would become the subject of Berlioz's *Damnation of Faust*? Could it be that Goethe felt he had made a grave mistake, when he was a mere twenty-six, to seek rest, comfort and an easy life in Karl's employment at Saxco, therefore sacrificing his independence, rather than to remain a struggling, restless freelancer? Did he believe he should have continued the life of the uneasy, brilliantly striving searcher rather than become an Olympian monument, a global celebrity?

Another question arises. Didn't both Faust and Mephisto represent aspects of the anti-human computer technology which, some will remember, Goethe mentioned in his published speech at the end of the Nobel banquet as the fortunate legacy on which he built his faith in living nature? In the film *Elegy* his intentions were clear – the villain was Lili's stepfather, the brilliant but humourless mathematician and computer scientist to whom the magician took such a visceral dislike. But in *Faust Part Two* the situation is by no means clear. Faust's everlasting striving and aimless intuitiveness seem to be designed to represent contemporary capitalism – unthinkable without high tech. Hence we have the term "Faustian Man", coined by some of our more pretentious journalists. At the same time, Faust was closer to the golden-green tree of life than to grey theory while Mephisto, the snake, was lurking in the lush foliage of the tree of life. His icy rationalism and love of abstractions were clearly that of Lili's stepfather's. Some will remember Gustav Gründgens' production of *Faust Part One* in which the rational Mephisto provoked an atomic apocalypse.

At the root of all these themes is the key question of man's relation to Nature. We all remember Goethe's speeches during the 'sixties, which made him one of the most admired figures in the environmental movement and the hero of Green Parties everywhere. It is clear that at the end of the twentieth century the situation appeared to him even more alarming than thirty, forty years earlier. Still, in spite of his acute concerns, self-helping Goethe is life-affirming and practical to the end. In the last act, Faust, nearly a hundred years old and at the point of death, at last discovers the purpose of his life. He is to clear a pestilent swamp and create space for many millions to live on free soil as a free people. Since he seeks to extend his own estate his motives are not entirely humanitarian and while doing so he commits atrocities against Man and Nature. Still, Faust "might be permitted to say" to the moment, the Perfect Moment, when he has achieved his aim, *Please linger on, you are so beautiful.* But please note that he was speaking conditionally. He said, "*might* be permitted." This was to prevent Mephisto from jumping into action and snatching his soul before our very eyes.

Always prepared to relieve darkness with a serious jest, Goethe snatched Faust's Factor X away from Mephisto's eager clutches and saved it through the use of a grammatical technicality.

And what does *Faust Part Two* tell us about the future?

When asked that question during his last year, Goethe usually smiled and gave his stock answer, "Let the future look after itself."

No doubt that is exactly what *The Goethean Age* will do.

endnotes

chapter one

For Goethe, evil had its origin in the cosmos and in its function in man. The cosmic force of opposition is used by the Lord to further man's positive growth. Human striving is continually reactivated by Mephisto's interference, lest it remain dull and inarticulate.

(Alan P. Cottrell, *Goethe's View of Evil*, Floris Books 1982, page 71.)

I believe that, unlike many of our contemporaries, Goethe would not have rejected psychoanalysis in an unfriendly spirit. On several occasions he himself came very close to it. Through his own insight he recognized many concepts which we have since been able to confirm, which earned us criticism and mockery and which he represented as self-evident. Thus he was familiar with the incomparable power of every child's earliest emotional bonds. He celebrated them in the Dedication in the Faust – poem in words which we could repeat in everyone of our analyses:
You shifting figures, I remember seeing you dimly long ago, and now I find you coming back again. I wonder should I try to hold on to you this time? Have I the inclination, have I the heart for it? You draw closer out of the mist. Very well then, have your way. The magic breeze that floats along with you fills me with youthful excitement.

(Sigmund Freud, in 1930, on the occasion of being awarded the Goethe Prize by the City of Frankfurt, reprinted in *Unser Goethe,* Diogenes Verlag 1982, page 927. *Faust,* translation by Barker Fairley, University of Toronto Press 1970, page 2.)

chapter 3

*The question that interests me now is this: how can anyone achieve such self-knowledge that he can create circumstances in which he can cure himself? Obviously anyone who can do this must have an incredibly weak ego, an ego overpowered, **flooded** by reality. In Goethe's early poems the concepts I and **the world** can no longer be separated.*

(Oskar Saalberg in the dialogue on Psychoanalysis in *Goethe: ein Denkmal wird lebendig*, edited by Harald Eggebrecht, Serie Piper, Piper Verlag Munich 1982, page 42.)

———————

In the afternoon, the Grand Duke's Library. His bust – easily recognizable. Massive chin and strong lips.

(Franz Kafka, *Diary entry*, Wednesday July 3, 1912, on a visit to Weimar.)

chapter 5

Charlotte could consider herself lucky that she saw him now and not fifteen years earlier, at the beginning of the century, when his cumbersome heaviness, which had began in Italy, was most noticeable. This he had shaken off some time ago. In spite of the stiffness in walking, which, however, was somehow in character, his limbs seemed young under the exceptionally fine and shiny cloth of his black tailcoat. In recent years his figure had began to resemble that of his youth.

(Thomas Mann, *Lotte in Weimar*, Fischer Bücherei 1967, page 260.)

chapter 6

Goethe wrote this poem on September 6th, 1780, on the wall of a room in the inn Lion in Ilmenau in the Thuringian hills, about thirty miles from Weimar. Fifty-one years later, on August 27th, 1831, a day before his last birthday, he went back.
Goethe read these few lines, and tears ran down his cheeks. Very slowly he drew his snow-white handkerchief from the pocket of his dark brown coat, dried his eyes and said in a sad, gentle voice: "Yes: wait, you too shall rest before long!" He was silent for half a minute, gazed once more through the window into the dark pine wood and then turned to me and said "Let's go now".

(J. Ch. Mahr, Inspector of Mines, Ilmenau, quoted in *Conversations and Encounters,* edited by David Luke and Robert Pick, Henry Regnery Company, Chicago 1966, page 237.)

chapter 9

The egoism of genius, which Goethe worshippers often label "sacred", shielded him from ordinary, every-day unpleasant-ness and discomfort. Even in wartime – for example in 1792, during the campaign in France – he had his servant carry him across puddles...He did not wish to hear about death and dying. His considerate lady-friend Charlotte von Stein gave orders shortly before her death that her funeral procession make a detour on the way to the cemetery in order not to pass his house and disturb him.

"Treibt nur Eure Künste", *Der Spiegel,* 43/1990, page 296.

In Goethe, 1749 years after Christ, someone had finally been born who did not allow himself to be distracted by the Beyond and therefore would not just live with whatever happened to him in this world. He did not fall for the line about King and Country, either. He did not proclaim human rights, he lived them.

(Martin Walser, Things Go Better with Goethe, *New York Times Book Review*, March 2, 1986.)

chapter 11

In a sense he [Goethe] only describes solutions. But since there is little suspense in solutions, and in order to satisfy our need for entertainment, he allows the solutions to emerge out of conflicts...Perhaps he was full of solutions for which he then found conflicts.

(Martin Walser, *Goethe's Anziehungskraft,* Universitätsverlag Konstanz 1983, page 29.)

chapter 12

Goethe was proud and arrogant but his great gifts did not entitle him to any pride, because he lacked the only gifts which justify pride – courage and greatness of spirit. And is one a poet if one has no courage? Truth and beauty are enchanted [verzauberte] princesses. One has to slay many a giant and dragon, one has to go through fire and water, one has to ride on horseback along a wire, to save and redeem her. But Goethe was no poet, he was never married to the muse; she was his whore, she gave herself to him for money and luxuries, and the children of his spirit are bastards.

(Ludwig Börne, Goethe's Briefwechsel mit einem Kind, from *Ludwig Börne, Spiegelbild des Lebens*, edited by Marcel Reich-Ranicki, Insel Taschenbuch 1578, 1977, page 119.)

chapter 13

In science as in art, the world since Goethe's day has gone the way he warned against...Art has withdrawn from the immediately real into the interior of the human soul, while science has taken the step into abstraction, has conquered the huge expanse of modern technology and has pushed on to the primal structures of biology and the ground forms that corresponds in modern science to the Platonic solids. At the same time, the dangers have become fully as threatening as Goethe foresaw. We have in mind, for example, the soulless depersonalization of labour, the absurdity of modern armaments, the flight into insanity that took the form of a political movement. The Devil is a powerful fellow. But the lucid region we spoke of earlier in connection with romantic music which Goethe was able to discern throughout all nature, has also become visible in modern science, at the point where it yields intimations of the mighty unity in the ordering of the world. Even today we can still learn from Goethe that we should not let everything else atrophy in favour of the one organ of rational analysis; that it is a matter, rather, of seizing upon reality with all the organs that are given to us, and trusting that this reality will then also reflect the essence of things, the "one, the good, and the true".

Werner Heisenberg, Goethe's View of Nature and the World of Science and Technology, in Across the Frontiers, translated by Peter Heath, Harper & Row, New York 1974, page 141.

Werner Heisenberg was awarded the Nobel Prize for Physics in 1932 for his work in theoretical atomic physics. He was the originator of the "Uncertainty Principle", which explains the impossibility of knowing exactly *where something is and how fast it is moving.*

197

chapter 15

The unholy alliance of unbridled power and cunning intellect nourishes the blind fanaticism which demands absolute control of everything in sight.
Man begins to act as though he were a machine, devoid of feeling and rumbling along according to inherent laws of mechanics, mindlessly grinding to dust whatever lies in its way. He is no longer human. He has become a monster, part beast, part machine.

(Alan Cottrell, *Goethe's View of Evil,* Floris Books 1982, page 144, referring to Act V of *Faust Part Two.*)

Boyle shows the place of Goethe's strangely fascinating theories of botany, geology and colour. (They seem to be the sources of modern "holism'). He observed with characteristic finesse that it was Goethe's scientific work (the search for an "Ariadne's thread" in Nature) that paradoxically demonstrated how his religious impulse (after he angrily rejected Christianity) reemerged in the quest for principles of growth, harmony and unity. "The underlying structure of Goethe's unwearying argument for a new chromatics [science of colours] is that of a defence of Arianism – the heretical belief that Christ was not divine – against the tyrannical sophistries of the established Trinitarian Christology. Light is tortured, indeed crucified, with the instruments of the scientists who...endeavour to split up the pure simplicity of divinity into seven colours or three persons or some other magical number..."

(Richard Holmes in a review of *Goethe The Poet and the Age: Volume One: The Poetry of Desire (1749–1790),* by Nicholas Boyle, Oxford University Press 1991, in *New Review of Books,* October 24, 1991.)

chapter 18

The distinction to which Goethe attaches such importance here, between immediate intuition and merely rational deduction, corresponds pretty closely, no doubt, to the distinction between two types of knowledge, **episteme** *and* **dianoia***, in the philosophy of Plato.* **Episteme** *is precisely that immediate awareness at which one can halt and behind which there is no need to seek anything further.* **Dianoia** *is the ability to analyse, in detail, the result of logical deduction. It is also apparent in Plato that only* **episteme***, the first kind of knowledge, furnishes the connection with the true, the essentially real, with the world of values, whereas* **dianoia** *yields knowledge, indeed, but knowledge merely devoid of values.*

(Werner Heisenberg, Goethe's View of Nature and the World of Science and Technology, in *Across the Frontiers,* translated by Peter Heath, Harper & Row, New York 1974, page 137.)

———————

Goethe's sensuality, his joy in sensual pleasures, is his strength. That, more than anything else, gives his work incomparable width and depth.

Richard Friedenthal, quoted by Rudolf Augstein in *Der Spiegel,* Nr. 18/1964, page 212.

chapter 20

What irks me in many of Goethe's biographers is their reductive tendency where his love relations and sexual attitudes are concerned. For example, did he sometimes take flight from woman? Yes, he did. But was it always he who took flight? No, it wasn't. Sometimes **he** *was rejected.*

(Elizabeth M. Wilkinson, Sexual Attitudes in Goethe's Life and Works, in *Goethe Revisited,* John Calder, London 1984, page 171.)

In the ***Elective Affinities*** resignation is practised even more drastically, leading to death by starvation. Ottilie becomes a martyr...In ***Wilhelm Meister's Years of Wandering,*** there are many examples of perfect self sacrifice. Makarie is a veritable coloratura artist in resignation...There is a flowering of peace-making, so that no conflict can ever arise again.

(Martin Walser, *Goethe's Anziehungskraft,* Universitätsverlag Konstanz 1983, page 40.)